THE NEW TENANTS

THE
NEW TENANTS

Margaret MacPherson

Illustrated by Shirley Hughes

HARCOURT, BRACE & WORLD, INC.

NEW YORK

Contents

25997

1

The New Tenants

"They're sure to be boys, aren't they?" said Sandy Macdonald.

"How do I know?" retorted his brother Hamish. "There's nothing to stop them being girls."

But Sandy was naturally optimistic. He dismissed his brother's suggestion as ridiculous. "Och, away! Six girls, never a fear of it! Well, maybe there might be one girl among them or even two, but even at that there'd still be four boys—" But here he stopped short, for he found himself addressing thin air as Hamish had scampered off with the ball. Sandy raced after him over the tussocks and hollows that made playing on that ground more than usually difficult. As soon as he was once more within earshot, he resumed exactly where he had left off.

"And that makes nine!"

Hamish, blowing on his cold fingers, frowned. "How on earth does it make nine?"

"With Ian and Murdo and Donald John, of course!"

"They're all away!"

"Murdo and Donald John get home for half term, and Ian's home for the holidays," persisted Sandy.

Yes, that was true. Murdo and Donald John had come home at half term. Hamish had looked forward to it for ages; he had missed Donald John badly. But everything had been different. He had hardly seen D.J. alone. Murdo and he were always together, sharing jokes and catchwords, brushing aside his attempts to join in. Just for a minute, while Sandy hunted for the ball, he wondered whether there'd be a boy in the new tenant's family with whom he could be friends.

Sandy came puffing back, exclaiming, "We could play four-a-sides—"

But Hamish was tired of all this speculation, which had been going on ever since they learned that strangers were coming to old Fergus Mackay's croft, which lay to the north of theirs in the township of Paible.

"Give it a rest, for Pete's sake," he begged, "and play if you're playing. They're coming today anyway, so we'll know soon enough. Oh, there's Mother calling. Come on!"

Their mother, a plump, pleasant-looking woman, was tying the end of a scarf under her chin.

"There you are!" she said. "Take the coal, Hamish, and Sandy can carry the basket. I've put in butter and eggs, sugar and tea, and a clothful of scones. Be careful, Sandy, and don't break the eggs."

"Little Red Riding Hood!" scoffed Hamish.

"Leave your brother alone!" begged his mother. "I'll take a bag of peats. What a day to come to a new home on!

If they'd only let me know earlier, I'd have had the house scrubbed for them. Take the broom, Sandy."

"Why can't Dad take us in the car?" grumbled Sandy.

"You know very well your dad can't leave the post office." Their father was the sub-postmaster, and the office was in an annex of their house.

Hamish had already set off. When there was something disagreeable to be done, he found it better to do it quickly and get it over. This walk was going to be disagreeable all right. At first they had the shelter of the brae with its birch, hazel, and rowan trees, but once at the top, the icy blast of the north wind blew straight in their faces. They bent their heads and hurried on, crossing a rushing stream by a plank bridge. Hamish set down the bucket to rest his aching arm for a minute. The sea to his left was dark and threatening under a rack of scudding clouds. The short winter daylight was fading fast. Ahead he could now see old Fergus's house built on a bare knoll exposed to every wind that blew. The old man had left it to a grandnephew in Glasgow. "That'll be another house only used in the holidays and a good croft going waste!" the crofters had predicted, ruminating over the matter around their peat fires at night.

But this prediction had been proved wrong. The Shearers were going to settle and work the croft. Rumor had it that there was a big family.

Sandy and his mother caught up with Hamish. "Hurry on, boys," she urged, "or the shower will catch us." Sandy whimpered, his hands red and swollen with cold. With a last burst of speed, they got inside the ramshackle porch just as hailstones hit the corrugated iron roof with a noise like gunfire.

"Oh, good life, we were lucky!" Peigi Mhoir laughed, lowering her bag of peats to the floor. She set about making a fire in the open grate. The room they had entered might have been nice enough at one time, but the once cream-colored paint had turned a dirty yellow with age. The ceiling was black with soot. Mice had made holes in the skirting board. A low-powered electric bulb shone on the neglect of years.

"Sweep the floor, boys, while I get the fire going." The kindling sticks began to crackle and spark, but a gust of wind sent smoke billowing out into the kitchen. "Drat!" exclaimed their mother. "There was always a blowdown with this wind. Don't be raising such a dust, Sandy. Sweep gently."

"The dirt's inches thick, Mum," replied Sandy with relish, raising another miniature dust storm. His mother took the brush from him when she was sure the fire was going to burn. "If they left Glasgow early, they should be here any time," she said.

"Ian does it in six hours," Hamish said as he stacked peats around the burning coal.

"He doesn't take six! He's fast," cried Sandy, and he ran around the kitchen imitating a racing driver.

"That should keep it going for a good while, Hamish," his mother said, admiring his handiwork, "and maybe heat the place a wee bit. It could do with it. Well, we'd better be off before it gets too dark to see the path."

The boys ran out. Their mother paused to lock the door, and as she did so, a figure loomed up in the twilight.

"Oh, good life, Danny!" Peigi Mhoir exclaimed. "You gave me a fright! Are you out without a coat on a night like this?"

The man poked his long, lean face close to hers. "Aye, a wild night and getting worse it is. Are they coming?"

She nodded. "And I wouldn't like to be in *her* shoes coming to a bare house with a parcel of bairns. I'll just leave the key in the lock." She was turning away when a thought struck her. "Oh, Danny, if you're visiting Hector, maybe you wouldn't mind putting a peat or two on the fire later on if they don't come soon."

"The ferry's off," he told her. "They'll be late."

"Oh dear, poor things! Well, have a look in, Danny, for it'll be a bleak house if the fire's out." With that she gathered her gear and took the shortcut home. Danny waited till the darkness had swallowed her up before—with a stealthy look all around—going inside.

Hours later the Shearers arrived. Mrs. Shearer took one look at the kitchen, sat down on a packing case, and dissolved into tears. "How could you bring us to a place like this, Dad?" she said, sobbing.

"Aw, for Pete's sake, Gracie," replied her husband, Fred, with a broad Glasgow twang, "a hoose canny look very grand—"

"It's not a house—it's a dump." Two small girls clung to their mother and sobbed in sympathy. Another girl, the oldest of the family stood a little apart. She looked anxiously at her father as if expecting him to wave a magic

wand and change the bare, dreary room into a comfortable home like the one they had left. Her father was a slightly built man, sharp featured, with bright blue eyes and a quick, eager expression.

"Aw, come on, Gracie," he expostulated. "It's just ye're

feeling tired oot. Liz, get hold of a kettle and make yer ma a cuppa."

Liz, the eldest child, was a tall, thin girl with a square face, a broad brow, straight brown hair, and her father's blue eyes. Thus appealed to, she set about looking for the electric kettle, but without success.

"Mum," she said at last, "can I look in the box you're sitting on?"

But her mother shook her head. "Dishes," she said, sniffing and blowing her nose. "The kettle's in a box *labeled*."

Good, thought Liz, she'd know it when she saw it. But then just suppose it was the very last thing to come in! Already a pile of furniture and boxes had been brought in. All the time the wind moaned and shrieked through the open doors like a soul in torment.

"Shut that door, Liz!" her mother begged at intervals, but with the men coming in and out the whole time, it was impossible. A tall, redheaded man had added himself to the two furniture men. With the doors being open, it was almost as cold indoors as out. Liz searched for the sink and cold-water tap but could find neither. She told her father, and the redheaded man, pausing to scratch his head, said, "Och, there's no tap. He left the water outside."

"Wish he had," joked Fred, looking at the water driven into the porch by the wind. Liz thought it was too late at night to make jokes.

"The tap's outside," said the other man. "Aye, it's just around from the door, quite handy."

"Oh, fine!" said her father. "Fill the kettle, Liz."

But there wasn't any kettle.

"Mum," she began again, but her mother snapped, "Don't talk to me. It's well seen your father's out of his mind bringing us to a hole like this!"

The men staggered in with a big table. "Won't be long noo, then," shouted Fred encouragingly, but his cheerfulness did more harm than good.

"Long!" repeated his wife on a rising note, but broke off as her husband came back in with a tall, dark elderly man.

"Here's our next-door neighbor, wife, Mr. Duncan Macdonald. He's saying his wife wants us back for the night, seeing we haven't gotten the beds up yet."

"I'm sure we're much obliged," said his wife. But there was one more delay. The spring of the double bed had gotten stuck in the kitchen door. The men struggled, heaving it up a fraction here and a fraction there, but all in vain. The furniture men cursed and swore to relieve their feelings.

Duncan Macdonald disapproved. "If strength and skill have failed, cursing will not help," he said coldly.

"Wid ye like to pit up a prayer?" said the head furniture man sarcastically. He and his mate had been on the road since dawn, coping with icy hills and hairpin bends. There was an unhappy pause, broken by Fred Shearer who said, "Best leave it till morning—we're tired oot."

Duncan Macdonald agreed. "I'll take your wife and children in the car, and you can follow in the van; it's just half a mile. We shall be pleased to have you join us," he added to the furniture men.

"I've a good mind not to go," muttered the first, but his

mate said his belly was so empty that he'd eat with the
Pope himself if His Holiness asked him.

Liz, who had long since given up her search for the kettle, had been standing, feeling the weary day would never
end. She followed the rest to the car. One more steep hill to
climb, one more to rush giddily down, and they were there.
The Macdonalds' house looked and smelled like heaven to
the weary travelers. The big room they entered was bright
and warm. A meal was spread on the big table, the kettles
were boiling, and a large frying pan sizzled gently.

First of all they had a wash in a blue-and-white tiled
bathroom. When the three girls and their mother got back
to the kitchen, the men were already seated, their father
with the baby on his knee.

"Be sure now and take plenty," their hostess kept urg-
ing them, but there was no need, for they were all starving
and ate a huge meal.

"That was a bit of all right!" remarked Fred as he
searched for a packet of cigarettes and handed it around.

"I see it's all girls you have," said Peigi Mhoir. "It's all
boys we have. We'd have liked a girl among them. This is
Hamish," she went on. He had been sitting silently watching. "There's just the two at home. Sandy was wanting to
see his new neighbors, but he fell asleep. You'll see him in
the morning."

Fred Shearer eyed his daughters, who were blinking
like well-fed owls. "I like my girls," he said. "I wouldn't
gi'e one o' them for a' the lads in the world. But we'd better
introduce them properly, now we're fed. This one's Liz.
She's twelve, and she's got the brains, and here's Dorothy,

near ten, and she's got the looks, and this is Joan, just
eight, and she's a good girl, and here's Daddy's own chick-
a-biddy Nellie!" The baby who had slept peacefully for
some hours beamed happily, earning praises from the
company. The other three were exhausted. Their hostess
took them to the sitting room, where she had turned the
divan into a broad double bed.

The room was beautifully warm. Dorothy and Joan
went to sleep the instant their heads were on the pillow.
Liz stayed awake for all of five minutes, puzzled by something, she was not sure what. Then she had it! The silence! No traffic, no hoots or honks, no clanging of shunt-
ing freight trains, no sirens from ships on the Clyde. No
sound at all. How very odd that was!

2

Settling In

His mother was making ready to go and milk. "See now, Hamish," she said, "and wake Sandy or he'll be late."

Hamish went on eating breakfast alone in the kitchen. The visitors were still asleep. But he ran upstairs before leaving, shouting to Sandy to get up, he'd be late. "Won't," came muffled from under the bedclothes. Hamish regarded the hump under the covers with disfavor. If Sandy wanted to be late, that was his affair. The Battle-Ax would deal with him. He was just about to go when an idea struck him, and a grin lit up his solemn face.

"Sandy," he said. "Four new players!" The effect was instantaneous. Sandy shot out of the rumpled bedclothes.

"Four? Honest?"

"Four it is, my lad."

"Oh, cheers!" cried Sandy, searching for his clothes. Hamish clattered downstairs, but Sandy came hopping out to the landing, trying to get into his shorts while hurling questions after him. Hamish did not linger. He snatched the last piece of toast out of the rack and scraped the last of

the marmalade out of the jar. He reckoned Sandy would
have a soul above marmalade for that morning at least. As
he was swallowing the last crumb, Sandy burst into the
room, every hair on end like the quills of a hedgehog.

"Did you see them? What are they like? Oh, I wish I'd
stayed up! How old are they?" Hamish was putting on his
duffel coat and did not answer. "Do they look fast?" Sandy
went on, swallowing porridge at speed.

"I dunno." Hamish replied, grabbing his satchel.
"You'd better be fast, or she'll keep you in at playtime."

"Oh wait, Hamish! I won't be a minute. You haven't
told me the half—"

But this made Hamish hasten his step. Inventing
names, ages, and even running speeds for four imaginary
boys was going beyond a joke. He shook with laughter;
there'd be some row when Sandy discovered he'd been
pulling his leg. Sandy's temper was explosive, which was
why Hamish played tricks on him from time to time, especially after the sharp disappointment of finding that the
new family were all girls. He had wanted a boy to climb
with, but Skinny Lizzie, Goldilocks, The Dormouse (for
Joan's nose had almost been in the teapot at supper, she
was so sleepy) and a baby were what he had gotten. What
a crew!

Liz slept late and, for a minute or two after waking,
could not think where she was. Then she remembered.
How queer it had felt the day before, being wakened at
four in the morning and trying to swallow bread and butter when they were more than half asleep. The house, with
neither furniture nor carpets, looked strange. She had

meant to say good-by to each room, but even her own bed-room had looked blankly at her as if denying she had ever lived there. The street itself looked foreign, for it was empty, and only the electric lamps swayed in the wind. But Mrs. Gunn's cat had come through the area railings, arching his broad back and rubbing himself against her legs. "I'm going away, Gussie," she whispered to him. "Will you miss me?" Gussie purred loudly as he always did when she came home from school. Her father called, and she had to go. The journey for all three girls in the back of the van had been wretched. First one and then another had turned sick. They had reached their new home more dead than alive.

"Liz! Liz! Girls! Get up, breakfast's ready," she heard her father shout, and sprang out of bed. The cold air clutched at her and made her gasp. Drawing back the curtains, she saw that the window was entirely frosted over in fernlike patterns. "Dorothy! Joan! Wake up," she said as she put on the electric fire and hurried into her clothes.

"Lazybones!" teased her father. Peigi Mhoir gave her porridge in a blue bowl, and then she had a brown egg in a blue egg cup.

"Look at that, Gracie," exclaimed her father when he had taken the top off his egg. "That's something like an egg. The kind of eggs we were buying in Glasgow ye couldnae tell the yolk from the white!"

"Aye, they keep the poor hens like prisoners of war. It's no wonder there's no taste to the eggs. We'll be giving you a hen and so will all the neighbors. It's the custom here when someone is setting up house."

Mrs. Shearer was feeding Nellie. "That house!" she said. "I never saw the like!"

"The old man let it go when his sister died. She had it as nice as you please."

"That's how I remember it," exclaimed Fred. "My mother took me home for the holidays, and it was real snug and cozy."

Peigi Mhoir agreed. The old man had become queer and would not allow a woman inside the door. Some people believed he had money hidden away, and that was the reason so many had come to the sale of his goods after his death. They expected to find rolls of bank notes hidden in the stuffing of chairs. Peigi Mhoir laughed heartily at the thought. "One thing sure, they'd have to burn everything after they'd searched—"

"Did they find money?" asked Dorothy, who had come in and listened wide-eyed.

"Well, now, I don't know, dearie, because if they did, they wouldn't let on."

Their parents decided they would go and clean the house, taking Liz with them but leaving the rest with the Macdonalds. When they went outside, Liz saw that the house was a big one. Wings had been built on, porches and sculleries added. It stood close to the sea, sheltered by a straggly line of elderberry bushes all leaning the one way. Liz looked about her with interest. The day was bright and frosty. They traveled the road they had taken the night before, first climbing the steep hill and then running down to the empty house. Fred Shearer took Liz off to

show her the view. He was as excited as a boy, seeing his new home by daylight.

"There's two or three good fields between us and the shore," he told her. "No, that bit of the shore's no use for bathing. It's too rocky." Liz saw how the sea stretched to the horizon, sparkling in the winter sunshine.

"That's some view, Liz, not a lot o' tenement windows wi' the washing hanging oot!"

But Liz cast a sorrowful thought back to the close-packed houses and clustering chimney pots of her child-hood.

"There's an awful lot of sea, Dad!"

He laughed. "All the way to America! But look, Liz, how it goes winding away into the hills and how nice the houses look strung along it with their own fields round them. That's real bonny. And look behind you now. That's our croft all the way up the hill at the back till it reaches the moors. We're going to make a job of it, Liz. We'll have the best cattle and the best crops, just see if we don't!"

Mrs. Shearer appeared at the door. "Are you going to stand out there all day? Just look at this! If I ever saw the like!"

She referred to snow, which had drifted into the porch at night through the open door. The bedspring stood jammed as they had left it. Fred scratched his chin. At this moment an old man, tall and fresh-faced, came to welcome them. His name was Hector Nicolson, he said, and he was their nearest neighbor.

"Your uncle and me was great friends," he told Fred. "Me and the wife are right glad to see you. We've been missing the smoke from the chimney."

Here the redheaded man joined them. Hector introduced him as Danny Ross. "Ah, he gave us a good hand last night," said Fred.

The men now tackled the bedspring and soon had it shifted. Liz and her mother gathered their pails, cloths, and scrubbing brushes. "We'll start from the top. Take cold water, Liz, till your father puts a fire on."

The water was freezing. Hard as Liz worked, she could not keep from shivering. She had to carry the dirty water outside and fill the pails at the tap. Icicles hung from it, and below was a sheet of black ice.

Their father came up to say he was off to find a plumber and an electrician. Danny Ross, who was often called Danny Ruadh because of his red hair, was going with him to act as guide. "And the old boy said you were to go over to his house for a meal."

"How could I go to a strange house in this state?" asked his wife crossly. She had her hair tied up in a cloth, an old sack apron over a printed overall, but when dinnertime came and they could not make the kettle boil on the smoldering peat fire, she changed her mind. Liz was delighted to escape from the bleak house and to run up the short brae to the Nicolsons' cottage. She thought it looked friendly with its whitewashed walls and blue door. It was cozy and warm inside the little kitchen, and old Anna, Hector's wife, crippled as she was with arthritis, came forward to welcome them with a warm smile. The table was already set, and Liz feasted off cold meat and pickles, with slices of plum-duff fried for pudding. After that they had cups of strong tea, shortbread, and gingerbread. Liz felt much better and had time to notice the cat, a large tortoise shell, which sat by the fireplace, his back to the company. She went down on her knees beside him, and presently he gave a low, rumbling purr.

"Captain doesn't purr for everyone," Anna told her. "Do you like cats?"

"Oh, yes," replied Liz, and told her about Gussie. "He'll miss me and wonder where I've gone."

"We'll give you a kitten then. They're out in the barn with their mother—"

"I don't want cats in the house," broke in her mother, "nasty, dirty creatures!" Captain turned his amber-green eyes upon her as if to ask what sort of ill-bred animals she had met.

Anna saw Liz's look of disappointment. "She can keep the kitten in the barn, and it'll catch mice."

"Oh, that will be lovely," said Liz.

Hector shook his old head with its shock of white hair after the newcomers had gone. "The wife won't stay long. She'll be wanting back to the city."

"That's a nice girl," his wife replied, and they both sighed, thinking of their daughter in Australia.

Mrs. Shearer worked till it was almost dark and one bedroom was scrubbed to her satisfaction. It smelled damply of wet wood and Jeyes Fluid. She regarded it grimly. "Well, it's clean—that's all we can say for it. Take that rubbish outside, Liz."

The girl dumped the rubbish in a shed at the back. When she turned, she saw a boy staring at her. His hair stood up on end like the bristles of a brush. He took a step forward, saying, "Are you staying here?"

"Well, we're going to when we put it right."

"How old are your brothers?" was the next question.

"I haven't any brothers."

"No brothers!" squeaked Sandy. "Not even one?" He looked so comical standing there, asking funny questions, that Liz had to laugh as she shook her head.

"Oh, gosh!" she heard him mutter, and he ran off around the front of the house.

Her mother came out, saying, "Your dad said to take the shortcut if he wasn't back, and it can't be too short for me."

"It's around this way, Mum."

"What I'd like to see," said her mother as they trudged along the narrow path in single file, "is a bus with seats inside for us both." They pictured the city streets full of big orange and green buses rolling along, ready to pick you up and drop you at your own doorstep. "It's getting dark already here, but the streets will be as bright as day. I always did like the shop windows on a winter's evening." She sighed, looking around. "But, Liz, do you think we're on the right road?"

In front of them lay the plank bridge across the stream. Mrs. Shearer was sure it was not safe. They would be dashed to their deaths. If Aunt Emily could see them now, her worst fears would be justified. She had said over and over they were mad to leave Glasgow. Liz said she'd run ahead to reconnoiter. She soon saw the Macdonalds' house comfortably sprawled in the hollow below, and she saw also a boy scrambling quickly from a lean-to shed onto the roof. He ran lightly up the slates till he reached the coping. He groped his way along to the chimney stack, where he sat down, and taking an apple from his pocket, took a bite. Liz, fascinated by all this, now made out another boy on the shed roof who seemed to be searching for something in *his* pocket. Perhaps he, too, had an apple? But why did they eat them outside on such a cold evening? Was it a custom? A sharp ping on the roof showed her that far from eating apples, the boy on the shed was throwing stones. The first boy jeered; the other tried again and hit the chimney. The apple-eater shouted something, and the other boy—oh, it was the one who had asked the funny questions!—aimed and fired. This time he hit the target, for there came an "ouch!" of pain from his victim. Cheered by this success, Sandy sent up a fusillade of stones but was in too much of a hurry to aim carefully. Hamish, for it was he, slid out of sight, gripping the coping with only one hand. Liz imagined a stone striking his fingers and making him lose his grip.

"Mum!" she shouted loudly. "Mum, are you coming?"

The boy heard her as she had hoped. He jumped off the roof with all the agility of Mrs. Gunn's cat and melted into the dusk. Liz ran back to her mother. "What were you doing and me getting my death of cold?"

Liz said they had not far to go now and coaxed her mother over the plank. Soon they were safely in the Macdonalds' bright, hospitable kitchen.

"We made oatcakes, Mum!" Dorothy cried. "These are *mine*," she said, pointing out the best.

"I hope they haven't been a nuisance," said their mother. Liz cuddled her little sister, warming her cold cheeks on the child's warm ones before running upstairs to tidy herself. She ran into Hamish coming out of the bathroom, where he had been looking for a bandage for his hand.

"Oh, I am sorry," said Liz quickly. "Did he hurt you much?"

Hamish gave her a sharp glance. So she knew! But girls, as he had discovered to his cost, were not to be trusted. This one, although she sounded sympathetic, would tell tales like all the rest. So with barely a pause, he replied shortly, "Nobody hurt me. I fell and skinned my knuckles," and ran downstairs. Liz's feelings were hurt. She hadn't been going to tell tales—she never did. She'd often gone climbing in forbidden places herself, on washhouse roofs, in back courts, and along the tops of narrow dividing walls, and kept it from her parents *and* Aunt Emily, who was always asking awkward questions.

The pity of it was that she had liked the look of him the night before, sitting silently in a corner of the kitchen. He had a nice round face and gray eyes and brown hair and looked as if he questioned things as Liz did herself, without being able very often to find answers. She had hoped they might become friends, but they had made a bad start.

Three days of hard scrubbing and Mrs. Shearer declared the new house fit to live in. That night, the last they were to spend with the Macdonalds, Dorothy said to Liz as they lay in bed, "I wish we were staying here, don't you, Liz?"

"It's warm and comfortable and Mrs. Macdonald is very kind. Mr. Macdonald is a bit stern—but the boys don't want us, so I think I'd rather be in our own house," replied Liz.

"*He*'s always in the post office," said Dorothy, referring to their host, "and I don't mind about the boys. Sandy made a face at me, and I put out my tongue at *him!*" She dwelt on this with satisfaction for a moment and then went on. "*They* wanted us to be boys!" She went off in a peal of laughter.

"Boys!" echoed Liz. "Why did they want us to be boys?"

"They wanted shinty players—that silly game with sticks."

"Oh, is that it?" exclaimed Liz, light dawning. "We can't help being girls."

"Don't want to help it!" murmured her sister sleepily. "Don't want to get hit. I like being a girl. When I'm big, I'll marry and never, never do any work—" Her voice tailed off, and she was asleep.

Liz lay in the warm darkness considering the situation. Hamish and Sandy had wanted four shinty players, and four girls had come. She could understand their disappointment, but perhaps they could learn to play. It was just like hockey, only faster. No, Dorothy never risked getting hurt, and Joan was too young. She herself could have played all right. She could do lots of things boys did, like climbing and swimming, and she could run fast. But what was the use? Hamish did not want to know what she could do. He didn't want to be friends, so she was glad they were leaving in the morning.

3

Going to School

"Well, noo, this is a bit of all right!" exclaimed their father that first evening in their own house at teatime as, with Nellie on his knee, he handed down his cup for a refill. "Gracie, Danny's been telling me this croft grows gran' tatties. Think o' that! We can have our ain tatties at the end o' June!"

His wife sniffed. The potatoes in the greengrocer's at the corner were good enough for her.

Fred stirred three teaspoonfuls of sugar into his tea.

"I've been telling Danny all the things I mean to do, draining, and planting trees for shelter, and improving the pasture—that's the thing, more and better grass. He was saying it was fine to have someone come to the place wi' new ideas. He was saying that's what the place was needing. For all he's never been oot o' the island, he doesnae lack sense, does Danny. Oh, I near forgot! I met the teacher on my way home, and she's expecting the weans tomorrow!"

"Tomorrow!" exclaimed their mother, dumfounded. "And how am I to have them ready when we're only this day into the house and their clothes not sorted out yet?"

"Oh, Dad!" protested Dorothy. "We don't need to go to school *here*."

"Hey! Where do ye think ye are? In Patagonia? Anyway, Miss Munro's fair pleased we've come, for it'll put up the numbers, and they can keep two teachers."

"Only two teachers! They're losing all the advantages of town schooling," said their mother, who had never shown any great enthusiasm for it when they had had it but wanted to grumble. "There'll be nobody here to bring Dorothy on in her singing."

"I dinna ken aboot that— Hie, Nellie, ye wee bauchle, ye'll spill ma tea! But that Miss Munro—she looked as if she could teach the cows their alphabet!"

"They'd need awfully big books, Dad!" Joan laughed.

The next morning the three girls were ready in good time, wearing their school skirts and blazers. Liz's long, straight brown hair had been braided, Dorothy's yellow mop curled naturally, and Joan's was in a ponytail. At the last moment their father said he'd had word of a tractor going cheap, so he couldn't come with them himself, but Hamish was coming for them.

"Oh, Dad, you promised!" Liz reproached him.

"Where's the odds? It's no' as if ye didna ken Hamish."

Liz thought it was just because they did know Hamish that they did not want to go with him, or rather he did not want to go with them. But before there was time for further argument, Hamish arrived, with his clean school face and his hair slicked down with water.

He set so sharp a pace that Joan and even Dorothy had

difficulty in keeping up. Liz held Joan's hand as they trotted after their guide, the bitter north wind blowing in their faces. It made their clothes feel too thin. The ice in the puddles crackled under their feet in their thin-soled shoes, and Hamish strode on ahead whistling.

"Is it far now?" Dorothy kept asking him. His only reply was a shake of the head. To the town children, accustomed to school just around the corner, the way seemed endless. The road ran through the townships, but the croft houses were either above or below, at some distance from it. Liz wished that Dorothy would stop asking how far. Asking did not make the journey any shorter. However, at last, at a turn in the road, they could see the gray stone building just ahead, set in the lap of the hills. A bus was putting down pupils at the gate.

"Better hurry!" Hamish shouted over his shoulder, and broke into a run, glad of the chance of separating himself from his following.

"Let's run, Liz!" begged Joan, tugging at her hand, but Liz said no one would scold them on their first day. In fact, they arrived just as the classes were filing indoors. Liz, with her sisters, joined the older group and followed them into a large classroom. Everyone went to his own place, and the newcomers were left standing while every eye was fixed upon them. Here was the new family come to school at last!

Miss Munro came forward to greet them. She was small, stout, gray-haired, and brisk. She took down their names and ages, then sent a girl to take Dorothy and Joan to the other room.

"Now, let me see," she mused, pursing her lips as she surveyed the classroom. "Ah, yes, sit here just now, Elizabeth. Helen, look after her and show her what you are doing."

Helen was a thin, pretty, drooping girl who smiled shyly at Liz. "Arithmetic!" she whispered, as if it were a state secret and went to fetch a textbook, a notebook, pencils, and eraser. These latter Liz did not need as she had a well-equipped pencil case of her own, containing three pencils all beautifully sharp, a pen, a box of pen points, an eraser, and a pencil sharpener. Liz felt that things were going well and that she would soon feel quite at home in this new school. Opening the book at the right page, she saw that she knew how to do the sums and set to with a will. Sums were very soothing after all the turmoil of moving and cleaning a new house. The room was quiet, a mere murmur coming from the eighteen pupils. There had been forty-five in her old class. When she had completed ten problems, she came up for a breather and looked around. Miss Munro was dealing with another class, all boys, while a third class was working on its own as they were doing. Liz examined her surroundings with interest.

There were charts on the walls, showing butterflies and moths, and there were lots of drawings and paintings done by the children themselves. One was of a burning house, and Liz thought it very good.

"Are you in difficulty, Elizabeth?" Miss Munro's voice broke in.

"No, Miss," she replied, bending once more over her work.

Miss Munro came over and stood behind her, studying

what she had done. "Humph!" she said presently, and walked over to the boys' table. "Come over here, Elizabeth. The work of this class will be more suited to you. Sit here!" She indicated a chair beside Hamish Macdonald. Liz got awkwardly to her feet and, in trying to gather up all her possessions at once, dropped her pencil case so that the objects it contained rolled about the floor. Now she stood hesitating whether to pick everything up at once or obey the teacher by going straight over.

"Helen! Pick up Elizabeth's things," Miss Munro ordered. "Hamish, show her the work you are doing!"

Liz sat down awkwardly in the chair beside Hamish, wishing that she had done all the sums wrong so that she could have stayed with the good, kind girls. Hamish pushed an open book at her but did not tell her which exercise to do. The other boys just stared at her. The sums, however, looked up at her consolingly. She set to work once more.

At the lunch-hour break, Miss Munro told her fellow teacher, Miss Fergusson, that her new pupil pleased her. "A clever girl, and now Hamish Macdonald will have to do some work. He had it all his own way with the other boys without trying."

"He was always lazy," demurred Miss Fergusson, through whose hands Hamish had passed. "Do you really think a new girl will make him work?"

"He won't want to be beaten by a girl from Glasgow," replied Miss Munro.

On the way home that evening, Liz heard how her sisters had fared.

"We had singing, Liz!" said Dorothy. "It was lovely,

and we're going to sing in a festival in the summer. The
school choir won a prize last year, and Miss Fergusson
says we'll win it again this year since they've got me. She's
awfully nice, and oh, I've to learn Gaelic, for the songs are
all Gaelic ones. Morag and Sandra are going to teach me
the words."

"I'm going to learn, too," Joan piped up.

"Oh, I suppose so, but you can't sing solo like me!" replied Dorothy.

Liz was glad that her sisters were pleased; their bright
chatter shortened the homeward journey. It was just a bit
of bad luck that there were no girls in her own class. She
supposed that the boys would become friendly when they
got to know her.

However, the boys did not become more friendly. They
talked in Gaelic, and although she could not understand,
she could guess that they were laughing at her because she
heard their nickname for her, "Skinny Lizzie." She felt
painfully self-conscious, hating to look up from her work
and meet hostile glances. She wished heartily that she had
a desk of her own, particularly when one of the boys began
to jog her elbow when she was writing and to take pencils
from her case without asking leave. One day this same boy
spilled ink on her book. His name was Angus. He was the
tallest in the class and easily the stupidest, but he showed a
certain ingenuity in finding new ways of annoying her
when the teacher's attention was engaged elsewhere. Liz
grew to dislike his limp carroty hair, his long nose, and his
small eyes, which seemed to disappear into his head when
he laughed at some ill-natured trick he had played upon

her. Liz was tempted to complain to Miss Munro but decided that this would only make things worse in the long run. She must fight her own battle. She studied the other boys. These were Alec John, tall, lean, bespectacled; Jim Kelly, small and compact, apt to daydream and have his hair pulled by Miss Munro to bring him back to the matter in hand; Ian Morrison, red-cheeked and smiling, and, of course, Hamish Macdonald. Liz thought that she could have made friends with all of them, with the exception of Hamish, if only Angus had not been there.

Being wakened in the morning when it was still dark and knowing that the long, cold day lay ahead was the worst time of all. She lay wishing she could stay in bed forever, safe and warm, where no cold wind could reach her nor hostile boy harm her. People said it was the worst winter they had had for many a year. Chilblains made both her fingers and toes unbearably itchy by evening. Her hands were badly chapped because she had not known to dry them properly before going out to fetch water on frosty days.

Matters came to a head one particularly dark evening when the children were hurrying, hoping to reach home before a gathering hail shower caught them. Then Joan stopped because of a stone in her shoe. "Oh, come on, Liz!" cried Dorothy impatiently. "She can put on her own shoe. She's always fussing."

Liz hesitated. She did not want to go back to help Joan. Her chilblains were causing her misery, and she longed to be home.

Three boys jumped out from behind a rock where they

had been lying in wait. Liz saw with a pang of fear that
Angus was one of them. They were in for trouble! She ran
back, but the boys were there first. Angus snatched the
shoe, piping in a ludicrously high squeak, "I can't get it
on! Oh help, help!"

The other two, Donald, a brother of Angus, and Sandy
Macdonald, burst into roars of laughter. Angus pranced
about holding the shoe and saying, "Let me help you,
dearie!" over and over.

"Give me that shoe!" cried Liz. Angus immediately held
the shoe high over his head, shouting, "Jump for it, Skinny
Lizzie, jump for it!"

Joan wailed, "I want my shoe! Get my shoe for me, Liz."

"Jump for it, Liz," said Dorothy. "You're tall." Liz jumped, but she was not tall enough. Their three tormentors bellowed with mirth.

"We'll tell on you!" shouted Dorothy.

"That's all girls ever do! Tell-tale tits!" And the three ran around the girls laughing, while Joan sobbed, holding her one foot in the air.

"Oh, isn't she clever standing on one leg, the wee dear!" mocked Angus.

"Oh, stop it!" cried Liz. "You're not funny, just stupid!"

This made Angus change his tone. He grew fierce and came at Liz as if he meant to strike her. "What did you want to come here for?" he demanded. "We don't want you. That croft was my dad's. You're just a set of Glasgow keelies. We don't want the English here! You go back to Glasgow!"

"You're stupid!" Liz repeated unwisely. "If we come from Glasgow, we can't be English. Glasgow's in Scotland!"

Angus spat contemptuously. "Oh, is it, Miss? Is it really, Miss? Thinks she's teacher! Oh, please, Miss! Please, Miss, can I leave the room?" This made the others almost helpless with laughter. They danced around the girls in a ring, throwing the shoe from one to the other. It was like a mad "Cobbler, cobbler, mend my shoe" in the wild, dark evening, the wind roaring down upon them, both sea and sky a surly gray.

"Catch!" they called, and up the shoe went in the air.

Liz gathered her wits together. She was nippy and quick and knew that now she had a chance. Sure enough, when the shoe sailed over Sandy's head, she managed to reach it first and clutched it to her. The next moment she fell face downward on the road, for Sandy in his effort to get the shoe had lost his balance and fallen on top of her. She lay winded. Sandy rolled over and got up. She heard Angus shout, "Get it!" and knew she must get to her feet before they reached her. Fear for her sisters made her face the boys, the shoe clutched in both hands. Instead of the attack she fully expected, there came a sudden silence. Sandy looked at Donald, and Donald looked at Angus, and all at once, as it seemed, they were off, Sandy in one direction and the brothers in the other as the first hailstones hit the children.

But for the moment Liz was too astonished to do anything.

"It's your face, Liz," Dorothy told her, awe in her voice. "It's all covered in blood!"

"Oh, is *that* it?" said Liz, putting her fingers up to feel. "I didn't know."

"That's why they ran!" exclaimed Dorothy. "You looked so—you looked so wild, your face white except for the blood running down!"

Dorothy helped Joan with her shoe, and the three hurried on, the sharp pellets of hail hitting the backs of their legs. Every now and then Dorothy or Joan would look behind, fearing to see Angus coming after them.

"It's all right," Liz kept saying. "He won't come any more." But her teeth were chattering so much that it did away with the comfort of her words. She was not frightened. She was sure she was not frightened, but still her teeth would chatter and she could not control them. Thankfully she saw the light shining from their kitchen window. Dorothy had run on ahead, bursting to be first with the news, so when Liz and Joan reached home, they heard her saying that Liz had been brave, she had stood up to the boys and gotten the shoe away from them.

At this point her mother saw her and cried out, "Oh, Liz!"

Her father took her arm and made her sit by the fire. "Are you bad hurt, Liz?"

She shook her head. "I don't think so, Dad."

Her mother examined the cut on her cheekbone. "We'll need to get it stitched," she said, but when the blood had been washed off, it was seen that the cut, though it had bled badly, was not deep. Dorothy, excited and upset, was going over the whole story for the second time.

"Who were the boys?" her father asked. "Who is this Angus?"

"Angus—I don't know his second name—and Donald —he's in my class—and the other was Sandy Macdonald—" But she stopped short, for Danny Ruadh, who had been sitting quietly in a corner, had lurched to his feet. Everyone looked at him in surprise.

"Is it not my own boys!" he stammered. "Well, now, is that not terrible!"

There was an embarrassed silence, and then Fred broke it, saying, "Well, maybe they were only teasing the lassies the way boys will—"

But his wife broke in angrily. "Teasing! Just look at the child!"

Danny now took the floor. "I will belt them myself," he announced. "It is myself will belt them this very night. There will be no more trouble, I'm telling you, no more trouble at all!"

"Oh, just give them a talking to! That will do the trick!" said Fred, smoothing things over. "Boys will be boys—"

"Don't talk nonsense," said his wife sharply. "And the minute you have your tea, off you go to the post office and tell the other boy's father what he did. I'm not going to have my girls frightened by louts."

Danny once more assured her that his lads would feel the weight of his arm and sidled out of the door in the curious crablike way of walking that he had.

"Well!" exclaimed their mother. "What kind of family can he have? And what kind of place have *you* brought us to without one decent comfort and the children frightened out of their wits?"

"Aw, jings, Gracie! They could meet the like and worse any day in the streets of Glasgow, but I'll speak to Duncan Macdonald. Here, now, Liz, come and take your tea, and you'll feel better with something inside you!"

Liz smiled at her father, choking back any mention of her daily miseries at school, but in bed that night, when the others were asleep, she gave way to a feeling of desolation that had been building up inside her since that very first school day. Was there something wrong with her, something nasty about herself that she could not see but which the boys could? Surely, if she were not nasty, they could not treat her so unkindly. Once she had given way to tears, they poured down her cheeks as if a dam had broken. She wept for the old life, the streets she had known, the closes she had chased up and down, the yards and old rubbish dumps that had been her playgrounds, the wee shop on the corner where she had spent her Saturday pocket money buying brightly colored candies, the big public library where she had spent hours choosing books and where she could sit in an alcove in peace, comfort, and warmth. She ached to go back, to see her old school friends, to pet Mrs. Gunn's cat when it came up the area steps, to hear the familiar roar of traffic as it swept past instead of this empty silence. But it was no use, no use. They would never go back, never, never. She sobbed herself to sleep.

4

A Quarrel, a Plan, and a Present

Sandy got the worst thrashing of his life, and he howled and howled. Hamish, unable to bear the sound, ran out of the house and climbed into the hayloft. He could not stand hearing anyone in pain, and his sympathy was all for Sandy. He had not meant to hurt the Shearer girl. He had only fallen accidentally on top of her. That could happen to anyone. It had only been a game, and if the girls had treated it as such, the boys would have gone off home and left them alone. But trust girls to make a fuss and wring the last drop of sympathy out of their sufferings! If anyone deserved to be thrashed, it was Angus, who had thought of the whole affair. Sandy had only happened to be there, but Hamish was pretty sure that Angus would get off scot-free while Sandy was thrashed unmercifully. It wasn't fair, Hamish thought angrily, not fair at all. These stupid girls! Why on earth had they ever come to the place? As always when he was upset, things he was ashamed of came rushing up at him. He had gone out ferreting with D.J. one winter's morning, but when he had seen the rab-bit rush into the net, its eyes bulging out of its head with

terror, he had felt quite sick, and he had never gone ferreting again. It was a terrible weakness, and no wonder D.J.
had given him up and now preferred Murdo's company to
his. Tormented by his unwished-for recollections, he lifted
his head and heard the clink of milk pails. He sprang
down from the hay and was bending over one of the cow's
chains when his mother came in.

"Och, is that where you are?" she said. "I was looking
for you everywhere."

"One of the cows was loose," muttered the boy. It would
have to do as an excuse. His mother did not question it,
possibly because she recognized it for what it was.

"Poor Sandy!" she said. "But it wasn't right to tease the
lassies, and them new to the place. One thing sure, he
won't do it again!" Hamish did not reply. He could not
speak of the evening's disaster.

By the next morning Sandy had completely recovered,
was his usual cheerful self, quite ready to cash in on his
mother's unspoken sympathy to the extent of a small bag
of candy and a tart put in his hand when he was going out.
But Hamish was different. His feelings, once roused, took
a long time to settle. When the wind has died down after a
storm, a swell still sends columns of spray up against the
cliffs and booming into the mouths of caves. So it was with
Hamish. He still hated his father's cruelty to Sandy, as he
had hated it last night, with Sandy's puffed and swollen
face before his eyes.

He got away from the house as soon as he could and
wandered along the rocky shore in search of treasure trove
the tide might have brought in. There was a new moon,

and tides were high. The wind had been blowing offshore,
however, so there was nothing new enmeshed in the high
pile of wrack. He spent a little time skimming stones, but
like everything else that morning, the game palled. He
continued his way along the beach till it narrowed between
sea and cliff. He decided to visit his secret hideout, a place
he went to at times of stress. He and D.J. had discovered it
together on one of their explorations, and they had never
told anyone else about it. So now he climbed a sheep path
that wound steeply upward, skirting rocks. Three-quarters
of the way up the cliff the path divided, one branch going
on up and the other running parallel to the shore. It was
narrow, with rock above and rock below, but if a sheep
could use it, then so could a boy as he and his brother had
discovered a year ago. Then he came to the place where he
had to crawl under an overhanging rock. The first time
they had done it, they had gone very gingerly, wondering
what next, but now Hamish went ahead with confidence,
getting to his feet and climbing the last few yards up the
grass-grown bank quickly. He was smiling to himself with
pleasure at the thought of his tiny cave. The grin remained
fixed in a silly way when his eyes came level with the
cave's floor and he saw the oldest Shearer girl sitting there
cross-legged, for all the world as if she owned the place.

They gazed at each other, bereft of speech, for several
seconds. Liz was the first to break the silence. "I—I—
climbed up," she said. "Isn't this a lovely place?"

It was a friendly overture, but Hamish would have none
of it.

"It's *my* place, not yours. I found it long ago."

Had this happened even two days ago, Liz would have departed meekly, feeling herself an intruder, but since her fight with the boys, her back was up.

"Finding places doesn't mean they belong to you!" she heard herself announce. "You haven't bought it!"

Hamish felt furious. Here they were again, these wretched girls, poking their noses in where they were not wanted!

"Well, you didn't buy it either," he snapped, "and I found it *first*. You come here, and it's nothing but trouble."

Liz frowned. "Trouble? What trouble? You mean trouble for us, I suppose. You've all been horrid, yes, all of you. What did we ever do? Was it our fault we came? I don't want to be here! I think it's a horrid place, so there! And you're all horrid to snatch a shoe from a little girl and—"

"I didn't snatch any shoe!" Hamish managed to insert this denial into the flow of Liz's anger, but to no avail.

"Well, if you didn't, your brother did!"

But this hit Hamish on the raw, and he broke in, "He says he didn't. It was Angus, but Sandy got the thrashing. That wasn't fair!"

"Fair!" echoed Liz with scorn. "And I suppose it's fair for a great lump like Angus to snatch a shoe and tease and torment us and for you all to gang up against me, yes, you —five against one! That's fair, isn't it?" She waited for an answer, looking him straight in the eye, and Hamish was put out by this turning of tables.

"I never did anything!" he muttered, all injured innocence, but that did him no good.

"Oh, you're a model, all right! You don't do anything. Oh no! You just sit and snigger at the nasty things other people do. If you had been there last night, you'd have just stood there and done nothing, just let your horrid brother cut my cheek!"

"He didn't mean to—" Hamish began quite meekly, when suddenly the whole import of what she had been saying penetrated, and he boiled over.

"Me do a thing like that! I never would. You think you can say anything you like, just anything—!" He was too angry to be coherent. It was only later that he thought up all the really stinging things he should have said. Besides, he was standing in such a ridiculous position—his face level with her feet. He couldn't improve it either, because if he pushed on into the cave, they'd be squeezed up against each other. So altogether it was not to be wondered at that she had the upper hand of him. She swept on raised by the high tide of her own anger.

"Well, if he didn't mean to, why was he there at all taking orders from Angus? *He*'s just a bully, bigger than anyone else, so he can do as he likes. I expect you're afraid of him too!" Before Hamish could do more than stutter a denial, she was off again. "Oh, I know you didn't want us here, you wanted boys! Well, I'm glad we're not boys, and I'm glad you didn't get what you wanted, and I'm glad you can't play shinty!"

Then running out of things she was glad about, she favored him with one last glare as she pushed past him.

"Mind out!" he exclaimed. "You'll fall," for she was taking the slope at a dangerous rate. She steadied herself, gave him one startled backward glance, and then continued down more cautiously. Hamish climbed into the vacated cave and sat down.

"My goodness! What a temper," he said aloud. What on earth had he done to deserve all that? His cave—he had only said it was *his* cave—and it was—and she had come out with all that! And the things she had flung at him, that he would have stood by and let Angus—that he was afraid of Angus! That was a barefaced lie. He was nothing of the sort! Why hadn't he told her that he had gotten the better of Angus in a stand-up fight long ago and that Angus had never wanted to fight him again? Why had he just stood there and let her say anything she liked. Next time he saw her, he'd give her a telling off, just see if he didn't! It was

quite some time before he was struck by the fact that she
had managed to climb the cliff all by herself. He had not
thought any girl capable of that.

The row spilled over into school. Miss Munro took the
five boys into her room and gave them a talk on being kind
to strangers. She then dismissed all but Angus. He, his
brother, and Sandy were kept in every day that week. The
whole school was subdued waiting for the storm to pass.

Hamish found that he could not get Liz out of his mind.
Up to that time he had ignored her pretty well, but now he
kept thinking about her even when she was not there, kept
thinking of all the false accusations she had hurled at him.
He'd have to do something—he'd have to show her! But
show her what? Well, they could beat her in class—that
would be something. They need not have a girl—and such
a girl—always doing the best work and crowing over
them! He held a council of war, sitting on the wall of the
playground, explaining what he felt.

"I don't see how we can help it," replied Alec John. "She
just knows everything!" Jim and Ian agreed, but Hamish
would have none of it.

"I have a plan!" he said. "We're five, and she's only one,
so it'll do if only one of us beats her in every subject. Do
you see?"

They nodded cautiously and waited for what was coming. "What we have to do is to divide the subjects, well,
like this. Take Bible study—well, one of us can learn
whatever it is every day for a week, then spelling the same.
Someone else can make sure he has every sum right, and

someone else make certain he knows all the meanings in the English passage—"

"Good life, Hamish!" expostulated Ian. "We'd never be done."

"A girl from Glasgow! Of course we can beat her! She's just been first so far because we weren't bothering."

"The Battle-Ax doesn't need to jaw us!" grumbled Alec John. "We never did a thing to the Shearer girls." The rest agreed, but Hamish ignored this side issue and went on at his most persuasive. "It won't be bad if we all take a turn. Say it's spelling—I'll take Mondays; you, Jim, Tuesdays; Alec John, Wednesdays; Ian, Thursday; and Angus Friday—" But here the class went off in a guffaw.

"Angus can't spell! Not if he was to sit learning spellings all night! He always gets them all wrong." This was true, and even Hamish had to accept it.

"So that's back to you on Friday!" concluded Jim, smiling, and when the others saw the expression on Hamish's face, they all laughed because Friday was "revision" day, and the one who got it would need to learn the whole week's spellings. But suddenly he cheered up. "If I get them the first week, it'll be Jim's turn to start on Monday and get Friday the following week!"

"Och, this is crackers. There's no sense in this, Hamish! What does it matter if she does beat us?" pleaded Jim, but now the rest, seeing both Jim and Hamish downcast, were all for it, forgetting that their own turn would come around. So it was decided, and Hamish was given the job of making out a timetable.

"Do you think Angus got a beating from his father?" he asked Alec John as they walked back to class. Alec John shook his head.

"No, Angus told me his dad didn't mind what he did to the girls. Danny's had an idea the croft was going to be his, and he's got it in for the Shearers. You should just hear him running down the Glasgow man and laughing at all the things he means to do on the croft."

Hamish looked thoughtful. "I wonder why Danny thought he was going to get it?"

"He keeps saying Old Fergus told him so, but you couldn't believe *him*. If the old man wanted something out of you, he'd promise you anything."

Liz, meantime, had retired into her shell. She had resolved that if Angus joggled her elbow, she would joggle his; if he spilled ink on her book, she would spill ink on his. But Angus offered no further provocation. He did not like being kept in all week, and moreover, Miss Munro's eye was on him. He sat silent and sulky. Liz ignored him and the rest as well, for by now she had lumped them all together as enemies. As to excelling in class, she had never bothered about that. She did not want to be first, but she could not help finding the work interesting.

Outside school she had two sources of pleasure. One was the kitten that Anna had now given her. It was a tiny little striped one, and she thought first of all of calling it Tiger but then decided that the son of Captain should not be Tiger.

"Call it Lieutenant!" suggested her father. "A step down in rank from his papa!"

"Lieutenant!" murmured Liz. "It's an awfully long name." But, of course, it wasn't, for it soon came down to Looty. Liz would run around to the byre every evening when she came home to give it its saucer of milk.

"That kitten of yours will burst!" said her father. "I gave it milk in the morning."

"Oh! Looty's hungry, Dad. Just look how fast his tongue goes, and Anna says I can go for another bottle of milk at night, for Molly, their big black cow, has calved now and they have plenty."

Up in old Hector's house, Liz would report on the kitten's health. "I think it's warmer in the byre than in the house. If the wind's in the north, we sometimes have to put our coats on in the kitchen!"

Hector knocked out his pipe as he listened. "Fergus was always good to his animals. He'd see to it there were no drafts in his byre, and his beasts never went hungry when sometimes I believe he half starved himself."

"But he wasn't poor!" protested Liz. "Why didn't he buy food?"

"He hated to spend money," Anna explained, "except on the animals. They always had their oilcake and a nice place to lie. Thatch is far warmer than slates for a roof."

Hector nodded. "Aye, he went a bit queerlike, having no one of his own about him, but, man, he was a grand worker, and he'd thatch that byre roof himself right up to the end, and there's not a drop of rain comes in."

Liz liked being with the old people in their warm kitchen, and she got into the way of telling them about schoolwork. She was busy on a big map of Australia in her spare time, making pictures of the things found there. They were specially interested because of their daughter who lived in Perth, Western Australia.

"You stick to your books," Hector would say. "If I'd had the chance of schooling when I was young, I might be a judge in the Court of Session today!"

In Glasgow Aunt Mabel had always implied that her sons got on well in the world just because they were *not* good at school. "People who make the most money," she had been accustomed to say, "are not the ones who are top of the class in school!" Liz had been told this so often that she tended to take a rather dim view of her own ability. Now here were people saying that book learning was of great importance. Listening to the old man, Liz suddenly realized that this was what she believed, too. She used to leave the little cottage feeling happy and content.

Then one evening their father met the girls in a state of great excitement.

"I've got a present for you!" he shouted while they were still some way off.

Dorothy at once began to run, shouting, "What is it, Dad?"

Joan was sure that she was to get her tricycle at last that she had been promised in town.

"A tricycle for you wouldn't be a present for us," Dorothy pointed out.

Their father beckoned them over to the byre.

"Ooo—it must be big if it's in the byre. Do tell us, Dad!" cried Dorothy, dancing with impatience.

"You go in and see for yourselves!" But Dorothy drew back. "It's dark inside! You go, Liz."

Liz went in. At first she saw nothing, but she could hear something breathing, and faintly alarmed, she stepped backward, treading on Joan's toe. Joan squealed out, "Oh, you hurt me!"

Their father rebuked them for a set of ninnies. "It's a cow! A real wee beauty! Danny and me got it today."

"Well! I don't want a cow," replied Dorothy promptly. "Can you take her away, Dad, and give us something else?"

"I want a tricycle!" wailed Joan.

The surprise had not been a success. The two younger ones ran off to the house. Liz ventured back into the byre to peer at the animal and saw one large luminous eye. "But where's Looty, Dad?"

"Oh, he ran up into the hay. Think of giving him our own cow's milk now, Liz, and we'll have cream for Sunday's pudding and butter for our bread."

"What's her name, Dad?"

"Rosie—she's red, you see."

When they went to the house, their mother checked them at the door, telling them to take off their mucky shoes and not clart her clean house.

"So it's a cow now," she remarked dryly. "Well, what I want to know is, who's going to milk her?"

"Milk her? Why Liz and me," replied her husband as he pulled off his boots. "We'll learn in a couple of shakes, won't we, Liz?"

So when they had had tea, her father took the lantern from its hook, lit it, and by its smoky light Liz followed him over to the byre. She could see the little cow better. She was a warm red with a white patch on her forehead. She was standing at the full stretch of her rope. Knowing more about cars than about cows, Fred sat down blithely on the milking stool, gripped the back teats without ceremony, and the next moment the pail was up in the air and then crashing against the wall while he himself toppled backward onto the flagged floor.

"By golly!" he cried, sitting up and rubbing the back of his head. "That was a good one! She's a regular goal getter—should be in the First Division. You have a try, Liz. She doesn't like me." Needless to say, Liz was treated in the same way. Her father decided it was time to call in reinforcements. Liz was sent for Hector. Danny turned up of his own accord. The men consulted together and then brought out a thick rope, which they proceeded to tie tightly around the cow's middle. Danny went to her head and gripped her by the nostrils. Only then did Hector sit down and run a practiced hand over the teats. Presently they heard the swish, swish of milk hitting the bottom of the pail.

"Well! Well! If that doesnae beat all. A bit rope and she canna kick. Who would believe it?" exclaimed Fred. Certainly the cow did not move, but Liz could see, by the way she rolled her eyes and struggled to free her head from Danny's tight hold, that she wanted to kick just as much as before.

"It's a good way of making them stand," said Hector.

"I've had to do it for the wife when their teats were sore with cowpox." And Danny, not to be outdone, remembered heifers with their first calf taking a long time to settle. Listening to all this, Liz grew more and more nervous. Her father had been foolish to bring home so savage an animal. When they had bought bottles of milk in the city, she had had no idea what struggles went into the procuring of it.

The cow now became an added trial to poor Liz. Indeed, she came to fear Rosie much more than the boys. She could not quell Rosie with a glance, and as to shoving or kicking, why the cow could win any contest of that sort. Each night her father made her take a turn, and she sat suffering agonies of anticipation watching for the lightning kick of the back leg and the flight of the pail. Danny and Hector usually turned up to help. But it made no difference that Liz knew it could not happen so long as Danny kept a grip of Rosie's nostrils and the rope was tight around her belly. She kept expecting Danny to slacken his grip or the rope to break. And as to milking, why, neither she nor her father could get much beyond covering the bottom of the pail, and then Hector would have to take over.

"Och, you're doing fine," he said to encourage them. "She's just a wee bit difficult till you have the knack of it. Her teats are small. Och! But you'll get the hang of it one of these days!"

Fred thought that it had better be soon. Even his easy temper took a knock. The muscles in his hands and forearm ached and ached with their unaccustomed exertions, and still he could not milk her. But one evening when Liz came home, her father told her she was to go and try one of Peigi Mhoir's cows, one that was easy to milk. "Oh no, Dad!" she protested. "I don't want to go *there*."

"Why not?" he asked. "They've been good neighbors to us, willing to lend a hand!"

"When we were in Glasgow, we didn't need anyone to lend a hand—we managed very well on our own!" said his wife.

"We'll soon manage here, too," replied Fred.

After tea they took the path to the Macdonalds, Liz following in her father's footsteps by the beam of his flashlight. They found the whole family at supper and had great difficulty in avoiding having to take a second supper to please their hostess. They were obliged to have a cup of tea beside the fire, and Liz was given a big treacle scone. She would have enjoyed it very much if only the boys had not been there.

"We hear you're good at your books!" said Peigi Mhoir cheerfully, and her husband said it was a good thing that she had come because now Hamish was working at his books every evening, a thing quite unknown before. Liz blushed the color of a peony, and Hamish went scarlet, much to the joy of Sandy who stored up the occasion for use at a future date. Supper over, Peigi Mhoir bustled about clearing away food and dishes, and Liz longed to get up and help, but shyness kept her glued to her chair while the men talked and the boys stayed silent. But at last they were ready for the byre.

Inside the byre there were three black cows and one red one, all lying comfortably on straw. Partitioned off from the byre was the barn full of hay, while a faintly sweet smell came from a pile of turnips below the cutter.

"Put the stool for Liz beside Susie, Hamish. She's the easiest. Just run your hand over the teats first, dear, and then let her stand a wee while. She doesn't let down the milk all at once." Liz did as she was bid, although it was like sitting in the dentist's chair waiting for the drill to touch a nerve.

However, as the cow only turned her head once and then resumed chewing the cud, she relaxed a little. To her great surprise, she found she could draw a thick stream of milk from the front teats. She milked on steadily, her nights of practice on Rosie now proving their value, for when Peigi Mhoir came to look, she found the pail more than half full. "Good life!" she cried. "You're not needing lessons at all when you can fill the pail as quickly as that."

"Oh, this one's easy, but Rosie's terrible!"

"Isn't it a pity, now, that your father hit on one of the hard kind! But you won't be a minute learning now." This delighted Liz, and Peigi Mhoir told her father she was a good milker already.

His face lit up. "We'll be proper crofters when we can milk a cow!" he joked. He told Liz he was staying on for a while, but he would give her the flashlight.

"Hamish will see her home," said his mother. Liz was seized with panic. She and Hamish had not addressed a word to each other since the day of the quarrel. She could not, could not walk home with him!

"I'll be all right," she said hastily, taking the flashlight from her father, and next moment she was gone. But Peigi

Mhoir was not easy in her mind over the girl, so when Hamish came in from feeding the cows, she told him to go after her and see that she reached home safely.

"I've got my lessons to do," grumbled Hamish, "and the night's not dark—"

"The moon's set. Off you go!" replied his mother.

"Ho! Ho!" jeered Sandy. "Going after dames!"

"Don't you talk!" retorted his brother. "I saw you taking candy from Goldilocks this very afternoon!"

Having dealt with Sandy, he stepped out of doors and

stood still to let his eyes adjust to the darkness before
going quickly in pursuit of Liz. His thoughts still ran on
what he had said to Sandy. They *had* been sharing a bag
of Licorice All Sorts, with every appearance of being the
best of friends, even though five minutes later they were
quarreling as usual. In fact, both Sandy and Dorothy were
happy to have someone to quarrel with. It shortened the
long walk home from school. But things were quite different between Hamish and Liz; they had gotten stuck. He
had tried giving her a nod in passing, but she had ignored
this completely. Well then, what could a chap do? He was
willing, he admitted, to let bygones be bygones and to forget her many false accusations, but all he got was a frozen
look. At this point he stopped in his tracks, for there in
front of him lay a flashlight, its metal gleaming faintly in
the gloom. He picked it up, recognizing it as the one Fred
Shearer had had with him that evening. Where in the
name of goodness had the girl gone to? He cast about for
traces of her, noting the place where she had tripped, con-
tinuing along the path and losing all sign of her. He went
back to where he had found the flashlight and shouted,
"Hie! Where are you?" But there was only the sough of
the wind through the bare hazel branches. He shouted
again and again, listening intently between each cry.
Goodness, this was a to-do. Should he go home for help or
should he start searching himself? It was certain she had
not passed this point on the path, so she must be somewhere below. As he hesitated, he heard the sound of something scrambling up from the bed of the stream some
twenty yards ahead. The next instant a ewe sprang into

sight, checked all of a sudden when it smelled him, and
swerved away, bounding uphill. Something or someone
had disturbed it to set it running at that time of night, so
he shouted yet again, "Hie! Are you there?" Then he
heard someone fumbling and stumbling up the brae. "I'm
here!" he cried. "This way!" and he flashed the light. Into
its beam walked Liz, a sorry spectacle, face spattered with
mud, stockings torn, hands scratched and bleeding.

"What in the world were you playing at?" demanded
Hamish because he had been worried about her, but Liz
only thought he sounded very cross, and she at once put
this down to the fact that he had been compelled to come
out after her. When she had first heard him shouting, she
had felt so grateful that had he not spoken first, she would
have thanked him warmly. She had been frightened nearly
out of her wits when she had seen two slits of green light
shining right ahead of her, for she had no idea that sheep's
eyes could shine in the dark, and even now, when she knew
it was only a sheep, she could hardly stop trembling.

"Gosh!" Hamish went on quite unaware that he was
hurting her feelings. "If it was a dark night, I could understand you going off the path, but tonight!"

To Liz the night was neither more nor less than pitch-
black.

"Thanks!" she said in a small, flat voice. "I'll take the
flashlight. I'll be all right now."

"Well, so you should be. I could go anywhere without a
light tonight."

This was as much as Liz could bear—one more scornful remark and she would burst into tears!—so having got a good grip on the flashlight, she walked quickly away.

Hamish was left feeling let down. He'd done his best to rescue her, and she had not even thanked him properly! He walked moodily homeward, blaming townsfolk for lack of manners.

5

Fire!

"Good gracious me, girl, what have you been up to now?" was her mother's greeting. "And where's your dad?"

"He stayed on for a while, and I'm all right. I just fell and scratched myself."

"He'd no business to let you come home by yourself! You might have gotten lost!"

"Oh yes, yes! It's the easiest thing in the world," chimed in Danny Ruadh from the corner that he almost always sat in now. He seemed never to stay home. "There was a man to the north of this place, and he was coming home one night and went a wee bit off the path—oh, just a wee bit, nor more than ten or twelve yards it might be—and he never reached home at all! They found him the next morning at the foot of a rock with his neck broken—aye! and the rock wasn't all that big."

Liz shuddered in spite of herself. She had so very nearly done just that, only in her case a high rock, the Gask Waterfall. The noise of the fall had brought her to a halt a few yards from the edge.

"You get off these wet stockings," her mother was saying, "and I'll make you a nice hot cup of cocoa." Liz was delighted to be fussed over for once, and she came downstairs in her dressing gown and sat by the fire sipping cocoa and eating a thick slice of bread and butter sprinkled with sugar.

"Oh, Mum," she said. "I very nearly milked the Macdonalds' cow dry by myself. Wasn't that good?"

"I don't know what good that will do you. I know I wouldn't go near one of those horrid creatures. I never expected a daughter of mine would be obliged to milk—"

"Och no, indeed," murmured Danny.

"She's good at her books, always top of her class! Not that I hold with all that book work, I'm sure, and I don't know where she took it from, for none of my side was ever good at their books, not but what they did very well for themselves in their own line, you understand, but milking! And that's not the worst of it, for that cow's not safe, and nobody needs to tell me she is! Why, when I saw that pail, I very nearly passed out, Mr. Ross! If that blow had gotten Liz, there was her kneecap damaged for life."

"Aye, just that," came the chorus from the sofa, "a terrible thing altogether!"

"Oh, Mum," Liz broke in. "Rosie's been good as gold all this week, and nobody's holding her. Hector said she was just homesick, and now she's settled down."

But her mother poured scorn on the notion of a cow being homesick, then passed on to her own condition— alone all day long, with no one to speak to but the baby, unless it was the postman or the co-op grocery truck once a week.

"Aye! It's hard on you, it is that, and you used to city ways!" came Danny's share of the lament. Liz got impatiently to her feet. She'd go to bed and read there since Dorothy would be fast asleep. She said good night politely, but as she climbed the stair, she wondered why he had to sit night after night in their kitchen. It wasn't as if his company cheered her mother up. He usually left her more downcast than he had found her.

"I don't like him!" Liz said suddenly aloud, and jumped into bed. "I don't like the wisps of hair he drags across the bald part of his head; I don't like his huge hands and dirty nails and the shambling way he walks; I don't like the way he butters Dad up, saying how wonderful he is, and then runs down the croft to Mum—"

Here she opened her book and plunged into the story, which was much more pleasant than thinking about Danny Ruadh.

From that night Liz's milking improved rapidly. Very soon she was able to dry the Macdonalds' cow and, not long after, Rosie, too. She was exceedingly proud of her new skill, much more so than of being top of the class.

When Dorothy opened the door one morning, she let out a squeal. "Oh gosh, Mum, it's all white."

"We've had it all white before," replied her mother irritably.

"Oh, but this is deep—it's right up my boots!"

Their father went out to inspect and came in agreeing that they had better stay at home. Dorothy and Joan threw off their coats with delight, but Liz decided she'd go.

"Will I come wi' ye?" asked her father.

"No, I'll manage fine," she replied, and so she did, for

she had Hamish's tracks to follow, and these kept her from floundering into the ditch. There was no wind, and the sun rising in a clear sky made the snow glitter.White land, blue sky and sea—only the cliffs stood out black where the snow could not settle. Liz arrived at school flushed and warm. The school bus had arrived half empty, so there was a pleasant holiday feeling about classes. During recess the boys fought battles, snowballing each other. Liz would have liked to join in but lacked the courage to take the first step.

Miss Munro, happening to look out, saw her alone and tapped on the window. "Would you like to go and sit in the library?" she asked.

"Oh yes, Miss," said Liz gratefully. The library was a little cubbyhole at the back of the building from which they were allowed to take books on Tuesdays and Fridays. Warmed by an oil stove, the little room was stuffy but cozy. Presently Liz, having found an old favorite, *Alice in Wonderland*, sat down on a stool near the window and became absorbed once more in Alice's adventures that she knew almost by heart. After lunch in the canteen, she slipped back in and went on reading, till, happening to look up, she saw Hamish on the roof of the coal shed just opposite her window. She watched as he swung himself lightly down to the ground. He gave a quick look around and disappeared.

Liz went back to her book. All too soon the bell rang for afternoon school, and the pupils lined up. Miss Munro came hurrying along and began the usual search through her large pockets for the key to the classroom. But this afternoon, when she turned the key and opened the door, billows of smoke rolled out, setting the whole line coughing.

"Dear me!" was all Miss Munro said, and putting down her head, she disappeared into the smoke. Next moment she reappeared, wiping her streaming eyes.

"Can't go in there!" she gasped. "Hamish, tell Miss Fergusson to march her classes outside, and all of you go out into the playground."

Her pupils dashed outside, glad to be away from the smoke. The other classes came marching out in an orderly fashion but broke into a babble of voices as soon as they were clear of the building.

"Fire! It's a fire, fire, fire!" went from mouth to mouth.

The two teachers were talking urgently in low tones when Hamish interrupted to say he would go in for the coats. They were all cold.

Miss Munro eyed him doubtfully. "What if you are overcome by the smoke?" she asked.

"I'll put my jacket over my nose and mouth," he replied earnestly.

"Very well, but you go with him," she added to Miss Fergusson. They disappeared into the smoke, and soon coats could be seen hurtling through the door.

"Elizabeth, bring them here. No, children, you are not to go nearer!" Liz ran to bring armfuls of coats, scarves, and caps to the waiting children. Miss Munro suddenly exclaimed, "The register!" and plunged back into the smoke. There was a breathless hush. What if she never came out? But she did, smudged and blackened but carrying the precious school register in her arms.

"I'm sure we should send for the fire brigade," said Miss Fergusson plaintively, for she was turning from pink to blue in the frosty air.

"Bring them thirty miles for a defective chimney!" snorted Miss Munro. "There's a fault in that chimney, always has been. And I've told Mr. Gambol about it till my tongue's tired. This time he'll have to *do* something."

There was a long-standing feud between herself and Mr. Gambol, the clerk of works.

"The fire engine!" muttered Miss Fergusson when Miss Munro was out of earshot.

And the children cried, "Oh yes, Miss, do send for it, Miss. Oh, we'd love to see a fire engine."

Miss Munro came back, saying, "The children cannot

stay here—it's much too cold. Those of you who walk home, off you go. Phone the bus driver, Miss Fergusson, to come at once, and start out walking to meet him, children. That will warm you all up."

The playground cleared rapidly. Liz was buttoning her coat when she remembered the key of the library still in her pocket. She hesitated, thinking she should give it back, but Miss Munro had disappeared again. Perhaps she should put it back in the door if she could reach it through the smoke. If the whole place was going to burn down, it hardly mattered whether the library was locked or not, but on the other hand, if she were brave enough, she could carry off two or three books. It would be sad to let *Alice* burn. She stepped timidly into the lobby, and then, finding that she could breathe quite comfortably, she ran to the little back room. She took *Alice* and slipped it into her school bag. Since there was still room in it, she was trying to decide which books to rescue when she heard a slight noise outside and saw Hamish on the roof once more, but going *up* it this time. What was he up to? She watched his progress with professional interest. The climb was not too difficult as he had rubber soles. He was now up at the chimney stack and hoisted himself quickly to a standing position that brought his head level with the edge of the chimney top.

He thrust his arm inside and seemed to be trying to grip something. Liz forgot all about the books and stood with her nose to the windowpane, watching.

It was icy cold on the roof. Hamish tugged at the piece of turf that he had pushed down the chimney flue after lunch. His nails clawed at the edge, tearing off small bits, but the bulk of it remained firmly jammed. He groaned aloud; his right hand was beginning to lose all feeling. He took it out and shook it to bring the blood back to his fingers. He glanced down and saw Liz gazing up at him. Well, that put the tin lid on it! She'd go straight to the Battle-Ax. "Please, Miss, Hamish Macdonald's on the roof. Oh please, Miss, he blocked the chimney himself so it would smoke!" While such phrases rushed through his head and while he saw himself being thrashed by his father to within an inch of his life, his fingers were making one last desperate bid to haul out the incriminating turf. In his furious haste he leaned too heavily upon the turf, and with a dull thud it fell inward down the chimney. Well, he'd had it now! There the turf would be, in the stove, visible to the first person who opened it. There was nothing he could do but start for home. He let go of the roof ridge and slithered down the slates, which were cold as blocks of ice, until his feet caught in the gutter. One jump and he was down on the coal shed roof, but because he was half frozen, he landed more heavily than usual.

"Hamish!" exclaimed Miss Munro, who was making a tour of inspection. "What are you doing there, boy? Were you trying to see whether there was a blockage in the chimney?" Hamish managed to nod in reply. "Well, that was intelligent of you. I think, indeed I'm sure, that we shall find something (here Hamish's mouth went dry), but you know it is absolutely forbidden to climb on school buildings. Come down at once."

"Yes, Miss." He swung himself down and nearly fell at

her feet, robbed of his customary agility through fear and
cold.

"Dear me, you are in a state! You must come in and
have a cup of hot tea before you face the walk home."

"Please, Miss, I'd better go home, I'm that dirty!"

She viewed him. "So you are! Come in and have a wash
in the sink. There's a towel on the back of the door—and
then come into the sitting room." She took him as far as
the sink and then left him. Tea with the Battle-Ax would
have been intimidating at any time, but when he had just
caused such confusion, even to the extent of making school
close—well, it didn't bear thinking of. He ran the hot
water, feeling like a man going to his execution. While he
was drying his face, he heard Miss Munro calling him and
shuffled reluctantly into her room. There, right before him,
sat Liz, sinking her teeth into a huge slice of fruit cake.
Hamish felt his spirit die within him. Like watching a film,
he saw himself repulsing Liz at every turn and pushing
her out of his cave. She could have her revenge now.

"How do you like your tea, Hamish? Two spoonfuls of
sugar? What cake will you have, chocolate or Dundee
cake?" The chocolate cake was beautiful, covered in thick
dark icing with some lovely squishy stuff between the
layers, but he was so upset that he grabbed the cake nearest, the fruit one, and then sat unable to eat it as he hated
raisins.

Miss Munro poured herself a cup of tea. "I found Elizabeth in the library, trying to save some of the books. Both
of you have been most helpful and have shown courage
and initiative."

Liz was enjoying herself. She knew perfectly well what Hamish was thinking and felt it served him right. *She* was eating fruit cake with relish, and *he* was sitting, looking like a half-wit, with the untouched cake on his plate.

"Did you see anything at all, Hamish, any stoppage?"

"Stoppage, Miss?"

"Yes, boy, anything blocking the chimney?"

"Oh *no*, Miss." The wealth of emphasis might have aroused Miss Munro's suspicions if her prolonged fight with Mr. Gambol had not diverted her quick wits into another channel.

"What's the matter? You're not eating your slice of cake."

"I don't like raisins, Miss!" he blurted out, turning redder than ever.

"Then why did you take it?" she asked, but cut and gave him a slice of the chocolate cake. She refilled their cups and, when they had finished, told them to hurry home. She was going to try again to get Mr. Gambol on the phone. He had not been in his office the first time. "But I think the smoke has lessened considerably. Good night, Hamish, good night, Elizabeth."

Hamish, passing the big window with Liz, made a quick decision. "Give me a leg up!" he whispered. She did so. He reached the sill, pushed up the window, and wriggled through the narrow opening. Liz bent down and undid both her shoelaces. She then knelt as if in the act of tying them. It was the only excuse for lingering that she could think of, and it would wear very thin if Hamish didn't appear soon. She was almost beside herself with impatience when at last she saw his head above her. "All clear?" he asked.

"Yes! Yes! Do hurry!" His legs came through, and he slid to the ground. "Quick! Quick!" she urged him, imagining that any minute she would hear Miss Munro's footsteps. Together they dashed down the playground, Liz's shoes going "clop clop" because they were still untied. They hurried on until they were out of sight of the building. Then Hamish took the blackened turf from under his jacket and pitched it into the roadside drain. He let out a long sigh of relief—the strain was over.

"Your clothes are in a mess!" Liz remarked, looking him over.

"It was feeling about in that stove," he explained, "and, oh my goodness, everything's filthy! Inches of soot on the tables and chairs! They'll have some job cleaning up!" He laughed heartily, but Liz did not join in.

"Whatever made you do such a thing?" she asked.

"Well—it was such a grand day," he replied, giving the question due consideration. "Far too good to waste in school, and I wanted to go sledding. The snow's just right."

Liz looked puzzled. "But—but—we're *later* than usual!" she observed, pointing to where the sun had already set in a bank of purple and violet cloud. The first stars were visible.

"Well, you see," he went on, sure that she would understand when the case was put to her, "I had to go up the roof to get the turf out, and then it fell—well, that was when I saw you—and then when I was coming down, *she* saw me and made me come in, so that took more time, but even if it didn't work out just as I planned, it was a good idea, wasn't it?"

Liz began to laugh. "If you'd seen your face when you saw me! You thought I was going to tell, didn't you? You've always thought I was going to tell."

Hamish did not know what to say, so wisely said nothing.

They walked on. "And then you sat with that piece of cake in your hand! You've no idea how silly you looked!" Hamish hovered on the brink of being offended. Perhaps he had looked a little put out, but there was no need to dwell on it. She might admit that the scheme had been wonderful, even if it had come unstuck in one or two of the details, but Liz started to laugh again. They had come to a small stream spanned by a stone bridge. She sat down on the parapet, rocking with mirth.

"What are you laughing about?" Hamish demanded.

"She said—she said—we'd shown— Oh! Oh! Oh! Courage and initiative! Oh! Oh! Oh!"

"Well, *I* did—that's just what I did show!" Hamish asserted, still on the defensive. Then he, too, suddenly saw the funny side and began to chuckle. "Courage and initiative! If she only knew!" They laughed and laughed till they were aching all over, and then they resumed their homeward way. Liz's father was coming to meet them.

"Where have you been?" he cried. "Your ma's worried!"

"It was just a fire at the school, Dad. Oh, not a bad one, just a bit of smoke, and we gave a hand."

6

The Accident

Their mother was dishing out cornflakes one Saturday morning when she said, "I don't believe there's a plumber on the island, even though you did go to see one! But if I have to go on carrying in buckets of cold water from that tap, I'm going to pack my bags and go home, so there!"

"Tell you what, Gracie. Come along with me, and we'll visit him together. Maybe you'll get him to come quicker than me."

"And what about the children?"

"I'm sure Liz can look after them. She's getting to be a big girl now."

"With her nose in her book and the baby in the brook!" retorted his wife.

"Oh, Mum!" Liz protested, but her mother was thinking things over.

"We'll take Nellie with us, and the others should be all right, but mind now, Liz, take care of the fire, and if you go out, put up the guard, and don't let anyone play with the gas burner (they had this on loan from the Macdonalds), and if we're not home in time for dinner, you can

open a tin of corn beef—" Her mother went on giving in-
structions and warnings till her husband told her the van
was ready. Nellie was dressed in her little red coat and
bonnet from which her small face peeped back at her sisters as her father carried her out to the van. They waved
good-by and then hurried into the warmth of the house.
Dorothy and Joan began to play with their dolls. Liz decided to do the housework quickly before settling down to
read. But when she had tidied up, she remembered the
hens. Their numbers had been increasing slowly as first
one neighbor and then another arrived with a hen in a
sack. They were lodged in a small shed next to the byre,
and Liz now went out with their feed, expecting the usual
rush. Not one answered her call. She found them still hud-
dling indoors. She had to run in for a shovel to scrape a
bare patch in the snow, and still they hesitated, like unwill-
ing bathers faced with a cold sea. "Shoo! Shoo! Come out
of there!" she cried, chivvying them down from their
perches. You couldn't, she thought, become fond of hens.
They looked too inquisitive.

"Shoo! Out of there!" she cried with extra vigor, and the
hens flopped down on the snow, all save one who flew
squawking to the top of the shed, flapping and clucking in
a great state.

"Do without your breakfast then!" Liz said to her. "Stupid thing!" Tired of the hens, she ran to the byre to see
Looty, who was delighted to have a visitor and played with
a long wisp of hay in a most charming manner. Liz decided
she might as well let Rosie out for a drink, and while she
was out of the way, she would clean the byre. It would be a

pleasant surprise for her father when he came home. Rosie
seemed to be surprised by the snow and stood blinking in
the sunshine, so Liz seized the pitchfork and carried out
loads to the dunghill. She was just filling Rosie's manger
when Joan came running out, crying that Dorothy had
taken her doll, Jerry, and was going to throw him in the
fire and Liz must come quick and rescue him. Liz saw
Dorothy, who dearly loved to tease, come out, waving
Jerry by one leg, and dart past them up the road.

"Oh well! She can't throw him in the fire now," said
Liz.

But Joan was not satisfied. "He's mine! She's no right to
touch him! You get him, Liz!" There was nothing for it
but to run after Dorothy, and she was nearly up on her
when Dorothy threw Jerry into the stream. Joan gave a
heart-rending cry, Liz leaped to save the doll, and Dorothy
ran away, laughing. Jerry was soaking wet. Joan was in
tears and amidst sobs swore that she would throw Dorothy's dolls into the stream, too.

"We'll put Jerry near the fire," said Liz. "He won't take
long to dry. When my panda fell in the bath, Mum dried
him for me—and he was even thicker than Jerry." They
went home, and Liz built up the fire, placing Jerry as close
as she dared. He looked like a sacrifice laid out on a slab,
oozing water, which sizzled on the hot stone hearth. This
amused Joan, and she forgot her grievance. But Liz had
only just picked up her book when Dorothy burst in crying, "Liz! Liz! Rosie! Rosie! She's in the stream."

"Well, what about it?" asked Liz. "She can't come to
much harm there."

"She's upside down—oh do come!" Liz ran out. The cow had walked past the house to where the banks of the stream ran high. In some extraordinary way, she had indeed gotten herself upside down, and Joan burst out laughing when she saw the four legs sticking up in the air. But Liz realized it was no laughing matter. If Rosie stayed where she was, she would dam the stream with her body, and the rising water might well drown her. The children tried first to make her get up, but as the animal had no room to move onto her side and thence onto her feet, it was useless to shout at her. Indeed, the more she struggled, the deeper she became wedged.

"Oh, what can we do?" cried Liz, and then she remembered Hector. He would know. "Dorothy, get Hector. Tell him to come at once." Dorothy dashed off, and Liz stepped down into the stream to keep the cow's head above the level of the rapidly rising stream. She shuddered as the icy-cold water penetrated her jeans, but stay there she must. Very soon she heard footsteps and, lifting her head, saw Hector coming. He took one look and told Dorothy to run to the post office and get as many men as she could.

"Tell them to bring a rope, a strong rope!" he shouted after her.

She darted away, and Hector went to the byre for a spade. The water was swirling and rushing past her, and Liz could no longer feel her legs. Her hands were growing numb. She saw Hector tackle the bank beside her, earth and small stones scattering down, some striking her hands. Then his spade struck roots of bushes. Getting to one side of these, he came on rock.

"That's it, that's the way, lass. Keep her head up. They won't be long!" he shouted to Liz, but to himself he muttered, "Ten minutes to reach and five or six back in the car, sixteen minutes—or more likely twenty, looking for a rope and shouting to people to come—can we hold out?" and he tore into the bank with his spade, and the water surged into the narrow passage he had made just beside Rosie's head.

"Good enough!" cried Hector, the sweat pouring down his face, but the stream blocked farther down, surged back, and lapped the cow's black muzzle. Her eyes rolled in her head, and she gave a low, desperate moo. Liz could not bear to look and held on with her eyes shut. The next moment her ears picked up the beat of a car's engine. They were coming! She tried to shout the news to Hector but found that her lips were so cold she could not form words —she could only make sounds. But Hector had heard the car, and his face broke into a smile. "We'll do it! We'll do it!" he shouted, and then to the men who were piling out of the car, "The rope! The rope!" Four came hurrying with it—Duncan Macdonald, Murdo the Post, Danny Ruadh, and Hamish. Duncan took one end and Hector the other. Murdo the Post got down into the water to push the rope under the cow's body; Danny helped now in one place now in another. Rosie herself, as if with renewed hope, struggled again to rise. Slowly, inch by inch, they pulled her upright till she was sitting on her tail, looking as Dorothy said afterward like a cow in a nursery rhyme picture.

"Heave! Heave, boys!" shouted Old Hector. "Altogether now, one—two—three—go!" From sitting on her tail, Rosie came upright onto her four feet, but if the banks had not hemmed her in, she would have collapsed. Duncan Macdonald pulled from in front, Danny Ruadh pushed from behind, Murdo the Post and Hector supported her, one on each side, and in this fashion they struggled back with her to the byre from which she had sallied forth under her own steam such a short time before.

"Liz! Liz! What *are* you doing?" Hamish was standing above her frowning in perplexity. "What are you standing there for? Come out!" She wanted to but she could not—the bank was too high. Hamish bent down, took one of her hands, and pulled her around till she was facing upstream. She could see for herself now that she had only to take three or four steps to where the banks leveled out and she would be able to step onto dry land. She gave a half nod. Of course that was the way to go, but even then she barely made it because her legs did not obey her commands.

"Come on!" cried Hamish impatiently, and he took her arm and half dragged, half carried her into the house. The fire was burning bright, and she stood beside it with the water pouring off her, making puddles on her mother's polished linoleum.

"Go and change your clothes, quick!" ordered Hamish. She nodded, yes, she must go and change, she was messing up the place, but still she stood, incapable of movement. Hamish was worried and was just going for help when the men came in. Liz knew that it was her duty to offer them all a hot cup of tea, and she was trying to reach the dish cupboard when a big coat was wrapped around her and she was lifted off her feet. She gazed up at Hector trying to tell him she was all right, there was no need to worry, she would make them all a cup of tea, but her unruly lips would do nothing she wanted. She heard Hector saying to Hamish's father, "Get her into warm dry clothes at once and give her some brandy, or it's pneumonia she'll be getting out of it! Hurry now!"

"We'll hurry all right. You get yourself dry, too!"

shouted Duncan Macdonald. "It's the cow will take pneumonia I wouldn't wonder," he added to himself. This struck Liz as very funny, herself and the cow both down with pneumonia. Would they put them in the same ward, and when she woke in the morning, would she ask Rosie if she'd had a good night! She gave a half laugh, but her teeth were clattering like castanets and she was shivering all over, so it was not surprising that Hamish's father thought she had groaned.

"Won't be long now, lass," he encouraged her as the car plunged down the long hill to the post office. He carried her into the house, calling for his wife. She came running and clucked with horror when she saw the shivering girl. "My goodness! I thought the *cow* was in the stream, not the lassie!"

"Oh, they were both in—they're a pair! But quick, a spoonful of brandy and then off with those clothes."

The brandy made her cough and choke. Still coughing, she was hurried upstairs. She kept trying to say how sorry she was for wetting the crimson stair carpet, but no one heeded her. Peigi Mhoir had her undressed and into a hot bath to an accompaniment of, "I'd have let that dratted cow drown rather than freeze to death! These men! I don't suppose they even noticed you. And what was she doing upside down anyway? A fine carry on! Now you wait there till I find you some clothes. Is the water hot enough? Will I put in some more hot?" Liz shook her head desperately; she was already lobster pink. "Now isn't it lucky you can wear boys' clothes! My mother would have fainted if I'd worn my brother's trousers, but what does it matter?" And off she went, in her element dealing with a crisis. When she was dressing Liz in Hamish's clothes, she noticed her swollen fingers and toes and went to the medicine cupboard for a tube of ointment. She applied a little of this gently to all the sore places and bandaged the broken chilblain on Liz's little finger. Being house-proud, as she remarked later to her husband, was all very well, but any woman worth her salt would see to her children first. She then combed Liz's long, straight hair, wrapped her in a huge quilted crimson dressing gown, and helped her downstairs. Hamish, Sandy, and her own sisters burst out laughing when they saw her but were told to behave themselves—the child would have died of exposure if left in that icy water any longer. Duncan Macdonald and Murdo the Post came through from the post office to see how the lassie was, for, as Murdo said, although he was already late on his round, he could not leave till he had seen for himself that she was all right. They convoyed her over to the big chair beside the fire, and Murdo suggested a footstool to keep her feet from the drafts. Drafts, thought Liz! If they only knew the drafts at home, they wouldn't worry. You would think I was made of china the way they handle me! But she smiled gratefully, thanking them. Murdo the Post then went away with his mind at rest, and Duncan Macdonald retired to the post office. Peigi Mhoir brought Liz a bowlful of broth. "Just a wee sip for you till dinner's ready—a good broth is just the thing! And the trouble I have to get the vegetables! Five sons, and you would think they'd be falling out with each other for the honor of dig-

ging the garden, but I have to be after them for weeks before they'll put a spade in the ground."

"Gardening's no job for a man!" announced Sandy.
"Can I have some soup?"

"Well, when you are a man, you can do as you please
and take your soup out of a tin, but till then—" A noise
made her turn her head, and she cried out, "Ian, *a luaidh*,
what are you doing here?"

Liz turned to see a handsome young man standing in
the doorway. He had dark brown hair, blue eyes, good features, and a firm chin with a cleft in it. He came in, kissed
his mother, tweaked Sandy's ear, clapped Hamish on the
back, and then said, "Are these our new neighbors?"

"Oh, just that!" exclaimed his mother. "And aren't we
lucky to get such nice ones!" Ian shook hands with them
all, and then everyone began telling him about the cow. He
shook his head.

"A bad day to be in the water! She'll be apt—"

"To take pneumonia!" said Liz, finishing his sentence
for him. With all the excitement she had thrown off some
of her usual shyness. "And I'm supposed to have it, too."
She giggled.

"Indeed and I hope not! But was she not a clever girl,
Ian, to hold onto the cow's head all that time and herself
perishing with cold?" said his mother, but this was too
much for Dorothy.

"*I* was clever!" she asserted, her cheeks pink, her eyes
sparkling, "not Liz. *I* found Rosie. Liz never even knew
there was anything wrong till I told her, and I ran all the

way here, and I was ever so quick! It's a lot easier standing still and just holding a cow's horns—"

"No, it's not," Hamish interrupted. "It's a lot worse just having to stand and get colder and colder. She could hardly walk when she came out of the stream. You were warm!"

Dorothy turned on him, ready to argue, but Peigi Mhoir said they were both clever girls, and hardy, too, to save the cow and them not used to country life. Ian agreed that they had both done well. Then he went out to see his father, and the boys went to examine his second-hand car, while their mother bustled about adding extras to the dinner in honor of Ian's arrival.

Soon they were all seated around the big table, and when grace was said, Ian's father asked how his studies were progressing. He was very proud of having a son studying to become a veterinary surgeon, although he did his best to hide it.

Liz looked with awe at a university student. She remembered how her father had taken them one fine Sunday afternoon to Kelvin Park and how he had pointed out the university tower and told her jokingly that, if she worked hard, she might go there some day. She had always remembered the gray stone building standing among trees and the green park that sunny day, and now she was actually sitting beside a student. Sandy, digging into a tin of sweet biscuits after dinner, sighed and wished his brother would come home from Glasgow every week.

"If I did, you'd burst! Never did I see anyone eat so much. You'd never be able to chase a shinty ball!"

"He can't anyway!" said Hamish.

"I jolly well can!" shouted Sandy. "I'm as fast as you, only you're older!"

Their father suggested that Dorothy should sing them a song. He had heard she could sing Gaelic songs, and they would all like to hear one. Dorothy was delighted and sang one of the songs they were practicing for the festival. She had a good ear, so that her Gaelic pronunciation was almost perfect. Everyone praised her singing, everyone, that is, except Hamish, who thought she was a conceited thing and not a patch on Liz who never showed off. Liz, warm and well fed, sat feeling blissfully happy in this large, boisterous family. She caught Hamish looking her way and smiled at him; he winked solemnly, and she was happier than ever, knowing they were friends at last and that she was an outsider no longer.

Ian took the girls home in his small car and visited the cow. He suspected her to be feverish and promised to phone the vet.

Their parents came home at dusk and heard the whole drama of the morning. The vet came shortly after and gave the cow a jag of penicillin and promised to return the next day.

The following evening Dorothy and Joan went to church with their mother, pleased to have a chance to wear their Sunday hats. Liz stayed in to put Nellie to bed and to give her father tea. They were just sitting down to it when there was a knock at the door.

"That'll be the vet!" exclaimed Fred, but found Ian Macdonald instead. The vet had been called away to an-

other case, but he had left an injection, and Ian was to give
it to the cow.

Together they went to the byre. Liz quickly set another
place, took the loaf out of its wrapping paper, and put the
shop cake on a plate. Presently they came back, and Ian
asked for water to wash his hands. Liz poured water from
the kettle into a basin and fetched soap and a towel.

When he had dried his hands, he said he must be going,
but Liz, blushing at her own temerity, begged him to have
a cup of tea with them, and her father backed her up. Ian
had already had tea, but as she was pouring out a cup and
looked so eager, he sat down.

"How are you? No pneumonia? Well, you're hardier
than the cow!"

"I was only up to my knees," said Liz. "Rosie was covered all over."

"So you're learning to be a vet? And you went to the
school here?" Fred Shearer remarked.

"Oh, yes! I suffered under the Battle-Ax!" said Ian with
a smile. "How are you getting on?" he asked Liz.

She wished desperately that she could think of something really interesting to say, but as nothing suggested
itself, she could only mutter, "All right."

"May I have the sugar, please?"

Liz blushed scarlet at her lack of manners. Entertaining
people was difficult she could see, for when you were listening to their conversation, you forgot their needs. Her
father luckily took over and told the young man all about
his hopes of making the croft a going concern. Grass was
the thing in that wet climate, rye grass and clovers. He'd

tackle silage the following year, and he had been doing a bit of draining, for no one could get good crops from a sour soil.

Ian replied that draining did good to the livestock, as well, by doing away with the stagnant water in which snails flourished. The snails harbored the liver fluke that attacked sheep and killed them. Egged on by Fred, he told them the life cycle of the fluke, and Liz listened entranced. It was as good as a fairy tale. When Ian had gone, she pictured herself in a laboratory cutting up sheep's livers.

Shortly after this Sunday tea party, during afternoon school when the less eager scholars were stifling their yawns, the door opened and a small gray-haired man came quietly in, so quietly that Miss Munro did not hear him till he gave a discreet cough.

"Mr. Gambol!" she said, and Liz woke from a daydream. "Mr. Gambol, I've been expecting you for some time!"

"I've been very busy, very busy," he replied in a dry, dusty voice. "Burst pipes, slates off roofs—not a minute!"

"A defective chimney is more dangerous than a few slates off a roof, Mr. Gambol," replied Miss Munro severely, not relishing being left to the end of the line. Mr. Gambol did not reply but advanced on the stove that was giving out a pleasant heat. He pursed his lips in a gesture that never failed to annoy the Battle-Ax.

"Seems to be working all right!" he said.

"Today its performance is reasonable," Miss Munro conceded, "but tell me, Mr. Gambol, why it should have sent out clouds of smoke such a short time ago? We have only just returned the classroom to its normal cleanliness."

Hamish, who felt the question should rightly have been addressed to him, dropped his pencil and disappeared under the table in search of it. When he reappeared, he displayed his fingers to the class. They were black.

"Chimney needed cleaning!" stated Mr. Gambol.

"The chimney had *been* cleaned!"

"Not properly!" A slow flush crept into Miss Munro's cheeks, a danger signal her class knew well.

"I put it to you, Mr. Gambol, that this kind of stove is quite out of date. The narrowness of the connecting pipe—"

But here Mr. Gambol was in his element and went into so many technicalities that even Miss Munro was shaken.

"If I have any more trouble," she declared, however, "I shall write the Education Authority demanding a new stove. The blowdown in a west wind is quite insupportable."

Mr. Gambol, still on his home ground, declared that not even the most modern of stoves would be immune from this trouble, due entirely to the situation of the school building in the crook of the hills.

Teacher and Clerk of Works then walked out to inspect other deficiencies, and Hamish gave vent to the laughter that had been building up inside him during the interview.

"He wasn't as funny as all that!" commented Jimmie in mild surprise as Hamish rocked with mirth. The secret of the turf in the chimney had been well guarded.

"Normal cleanliness," he spluttered, holding up his filthy fingers, "normal cleanliness!" This gave them all a reason to join in, and they were all holding up their dirty hands and crying, "Normal cleanliness!" when the Battle-Ax walked in. Silence descended, broken by one last hiccup from Hamish.

Miss Munro stood looking at them, and the silence became so oppressive that the pupils twitched with discomfort. In an icy voice Miss Munro spoke. "Will you be so good as to explain, Hamish Macdonald, why, when I leave the room, pandemonium breaks out?"

Hamish got awkwardly to his feet. "Please, Miss," he began, "please, Miss, it was the dirt." As an excuse it sounded excessively thin.

"The dirt!" Miss Munro repeated. "What is funny about dirt?"

"Please, Miss, you said that the room was restored to its normal cleanliness, and please, Miss, it isn't. Under the table is black!"

There ensued another horrid silence. The entire room was as hushed as a church congregation. Hamish, still unhappily on his feet, forced himself to look straight at Miss Munro till he remembered reading that liars were well known to look people in the eye while the innocent hung their heads. He could feel a slow tide of red creeping up his neck and over his jaws into his cheeks.

At last she spoke. "And that was very funny?" It felt far from funny now, and Hamish had the uncomfortable feeling that she could read his thoughts and that, if this went on much longer, he would confess what had really happened on the first day of the snow.

"Yes, Miss," was all he could manage.

"I am glad to find that cleanliness so concerns you, Hamish. Stay behind after school and wash the underside of those pieces of furniture that have escaped the notice of the cleaners."

Relieved but also deflated, Hamish sat down, and work resumed.

7

Money on Four Feet

"Here's Dad coming to meet us!" cried Dorothy as the girls were on their way home from school on Friday.

"Come along and see the cattle I've bought!" he said, but only Liz was willing to turn back, and even she was sorry she had done so when she found that he was making for Danny Ruadh's cottage. A rough dirt track—much rutted by winter weather—led to it. The house was in a lovely place just beside the shore, and Liz imagined herself running out to bathe at any odd time, the sea so near, but when she saw the house better, it had an uncared-for air, the bare stone showing through the rough plaster, the coping broken, the windowframes bare of paint. Under a broken drain pipe stood a barrel full of rain water on which floated green scum. A dog came running up to them, alternately snarling and slinking. The din it made announced their arrival, and Danny came hurrying out, saying with all his usual cordiality, "Come in! Come in! You're a welcome sight." Liz followed her father reluctantly into the small kitchen, where a skinny, sallow-

complexioned woman, her thin hair in a tight bun, was
standing by the open fire.

"Here's our neighbors come to see us, wife!" announced
Danny. His wife wiped her hand on a greasy apron and
stretched it out. Fred shook it cordially but Liz unwillingly.

"We've just come for a peep at the cattle," Fred explained.

"Och! To be sure, to be sure, but you'll stay and have a
bite with us, tatties and herring—poor fare for town folk,
but you're very welcome."

"There's nothing I like better than tatties and herring,"
replied Fred, slightly offended at being described as town

folk, "but we're in a hurry today. You stay and talk to Mrs. Ross, Liz. We'll get the cattle."

Off they went, Danny, her father, Angus, and Donald, and she was left in the stuffy kitchen with a host of grubby kids peering at her from behind chairs. She wished heartily that she had gone straight home.

"We all hear that you are good at your books!" The woman had a singsong way of speaking, which hid an undercurrent of complaint. "It's fine to be good at your books!"

Liz wriggled with discomfort and found not a word to say. Her hostess continued. "The trouble we have with that school! You wouldn't believe it! They wouldn't give us a bridge, wouldn't hear of it, so how could they expect the children to reach the school and the burn in spate?"

Liz felt tolerably sure that Angus could jump any stream he had a mind to, and Donald and Peter as well. Of course it might be an obstacle for the little ones who were now staring at her so fixedly.

"It's a sore trial—no road!" the woman droned on. "We have to carry everything on our backs! Oh, the work it is —you've no idea!" As she talked, she kept stabbing the potatoes in the pot till Liz felt certain they would disintegrate completely.

"And how are you liking life in the country?" she asked with a sudden change of tone and giving Liz a quick look.

"Very well, thank you," replied Liz politely.

"It's a nice place you have to be sure, and so handy to the road, and the water in a pipe at the door!" Liz smiled a little thinking how her mother described the same house.

"Handy" was not a word she applied to it. Shortly after-
wards, to her great relief, she heard the men at the door.
She sprang up and, when Danny's wife offered her a glass
of milk, refused, saying she was not thirsty.

"You'll have a biscuit then, surely you'll have a biscuit?" Liz shook her head. "No, no thanks!" Her father
said she had better take something, she'd had nothing
since dinner. This caused another burst of offerings, but
Liz was determined not to eat in that house. There was
something wrong with it. She had never liked Danny, and
now she found herself disliking his wife as well. "I want to
see the cattle," she said. Her father shrugged and led the
way, and Liz was so glad to escape that she forgot to say
good-by. Outside were six small Aberdeen-Angus stirks,
shaggy-coated, with balls of dung sticking to their hind-
quarters. Danny and her father went around them, re-
marking on all their good points, while Angus stood a few
paces off, his mouth half open, which gave him the look of
laughing at something. Her father said he would come for
them tomorrow when he had prepared a place. Danny kept
murmuring that there was no hurry, no hurry in the world.

Liz walked fast to put distance between her and the
whole Ross family. She wanted neither to think nor talk of
them, but her father did.

"Why did you refuse a glass of milk?" he demanded.
"The first time you were in their house, too! It would be
mannerly to take a glass!"

"I didn't want anything, Dad," she replied, thinking he
ought to understand without having everything put into
words.

"Well, you're usually hungry when you come home from school!"

"I don't like—" Liz began, but her father interrupted.

"That's just it! You don't like! Well, let me tell you, Danny's been a good friend to me, giving me a han' wi' the tractor, putting me up to things, me being a beginner you might say, and now these stirks! He's given me a bargain. I'd never get the like at a sale. I'll make £10 out of each one by the autumn, you see if I don't!" And he smiled with satisfaction but then recollected that Liz was due a dressing down.

"You should nae set yourself up to judge other people, even if you are good at your books!"

Liz took her father's criticisms to heart. Had she been judging people—well, not because they were *stupid!* Being stupid didn't matter. It wasn't that—it was something quite different that you either felt or you didn't. Why even Nellie cried when Danny came near her!

She knew a momentary irritation with her father because he did not feel it. She was still trying to find words when they fell in with a crofter on his way to the post office for his pension, and the subject lapsed.

The next day the cattle took up a lot of time. In the morning Liz had to stand by with hammer and nails while her father made them a pen, and then in the evening came the difficulty of putting them into strange quarters. Fred Shearer had talked of putting stirks inside as if they were so many tables and chairs, but when he came to try it, he learned otherwise. The leading beast jibbed at the doorway and fell backward, jostling and upsetting the rest. Fred began to beat the one nearest, with the result that the whole lot charged in confusion up the road.

"After them, Liz!" he shouted, but they were halfway up the hill before she managed to get ahead. Once turned, they went galloping back down. Dorothy and Joan fled squealing in terror, and their father had his work cut out to stop the animals making off down the road.

"This is some do!" he grumbled, panting, his hair on end. "Silly sausages! There's a manger full of hay right there inside." But the stirks knew nothing of that and this time ran around the back of the building.

"Come on!" cried he. "We're not going to be beat!" and he ran around after them, but such rough handling succeeded only in frightening the animals out of their wits. Once more they rushed up the road, but this time they met Hamish coming down on his bicycle. He grasped what was happening and jumped off, driving them back once more. Hector, hearing the din, came down from his house and took charge. It was growing dark, and if the stirks were not soon housed, they would make good their escape.

"Take your time," said Hector, "take your time! The beasts are scared—just let them stand!"

So in the dusk the six small stirks stood with heaving flanks and tossing heads while the human beings stood waiting in a half circle. Presently the old man took the cow from the byre and let her stand among them. She sniffed and prodded them and finally decided it was warmer inside. Hector beckoned them nearer; slowly they closed in on the stirks till there was nothing for them to do but follow the cow. One! Two! Three! Four! Five! Then without

warning the sixth shied and made to bolt. "Close in!"
shouted Hector as he sprang forward and gave the beast a
sharp rap on its rump. With a startled grunt it plunged
through the door, which Hector promptly closed.

"Well, there's a right way and a wrong way of doing
everything!" commented Fred, ruefully rubbing his chin.

"Och, you must give them plenty of time, plenty of time.
Never frighten them, just take it quietly like."

"You moved pretty quick over that last one, though!"

The old man smiled and nodded. "Oh, aye! When you
have to move, move fast. When I was young, I could jump
for a running beast's horns and bring him down. Now if
that one had gotten away, it wouldn't have smelled the inside of the byre tonight!"

Liz chuckled. What funny expressions they used!
Smelled it! But of course it was true—beasts did become
acquainted with places through their noses. Hamish was
picking up his bike. "Are you coming in?" she asked, but
he shook his head. Go in there with all these girls—what
an idea!

"I'm off with a telegram," he said. "Come along to the
hideout tomorrow."

"When?" asked Liz. "Oh, in the afternoon sometime,"
he replied, as if an hour here or there made no difference.

"Right!" was all she said, but inwardly she was all of a
glow. He had asked her to his secret place! That was indeed an honor.

Her father was asking Hector to go in with him, but the
old man excused himself. His wife was making tea when
he left. But the truth was he never felt at home in the

Shearers'. The wife was always so busy tidying up. If he so much as dropped a burned match, she was down on her knees with a shovel and brush. He couldn't be doing with it.

"We got them in, Gracie! Some job!" shouted her husband as he and Liz went in.

"You've taken long enough"—she sniffed—"besides frightening the children out of their wits!"

"What were they squawling about? They'll have to grow hardy! It's a good thing I've got one to gi'e me a han'. But that's the beginning o' our fortune, Gracie! When I sell that lot, I'll make £60 profit and buy ye a fur coat."

"That'll be the day! All that money on four feet! I'd sooner have it in the bank!"

They all laughed. "Money on four feet" became a family catchword and the collective name for the six stirks.

The following afternoon being Sunday, Liz ran along the shore, sniffing the seaweed. The bite had gone from the wind, the sun every now and then broke through high-riding cloud, and a breeze from the south was rippling the sea. Sheep, startled by her coming, bounded away snorting uphill, and she herself took the narrow track winding up till she had to drop down on her knees and crawl under the overhanging rock. Once safely past this obstacle, she climbed the last grassy slope, and when her head came level with the floor of the tiny cave, she saw Hamish already seated in it.

"Oh, I was sure I'd be first!" she exclaimed as she settled herself beside him. "Oh, this is nice!" She hugged her knees as she gazed down on the rocky shore below. The tide was far out, exposing the long fronds of dark weed.

"Can you swim?" Hamish asked.

"Oh yes, I learned in the public baths."

"The sea's different," said he. "Could you swim between that rock and that one?" He pointed to two large rocks running out into the water about two hundred yards apart. Liz considered the question carefully before saying that she thought she could.

"We'll race it in summer."

"That'll be fun!"

"What have you got in your pocket?" was the next question.

"A book—I thought I might have to wait a long time."

"Who wants books outside? There's always something to watch."

Liz blushed faintly. "Yes," she agreed, "but I don't know what I'm looking at, and there's no one to ask."

"How do you mean you don't know what you're looking at?"

"Well, like birds—unless it's sparrows or starlings, I don't know them, and—"

"Oh, birds!" Hamish smiled, thinking it funny not to know them. "I'll give you their names," and he began the lesson at once. There were plenty of birds in sight—herring gulls and lesser black-backed gulls, oyster catchers and guillemots. He ended by saying, "I'll show you nests when we get our holidays."

Liz was delighted with this and said so.

"How did you get on with the stirks after that?" Hamish inquired.

"Dad and Hector got them into the pen, and we're going to leave them there till they settle. We'd never get them back inside by ourselves."

"They'll soon settle. I expect your dad will feed them better than Danny did. Why did he want to buy just now and not wait for the sales in May?"

"Well, he got a bargain," Liz explained. "He wouldn't have gotten them so cheap at the sale." As she said this, she turned to look at Hamish and caught a very odd expression on his face.

"What is it? What's wrong?" she asked.

Hamish was in a dilemma. He knew one should not ask straight out about prices, but he was eaten up with curiosity to know what Danny had gotten for his cattle, so after a short struggle he blurted out, "How much did your dad give for them?"

Liz did not in the least mind telling him. She was proud of her father and his ability to cope. "He gave £40 a head, and he says he'll get £50 a piece in the autumn."

"Forty pounds!" was all Hamish said, but it was too much.

"What do you mean?" asked Liz, frowning. "Was it too much or not enough?" But he shook his head and only muttered. But this annoyed Liz, and she rounded on him. "You asked and I told you, and then you say '£40!' like that, so now you've got to tell me was it too much or too little."

"Too much," said Hamish with reluctance, wishing he'd left the whole thing alone.

"Far too much?" Liz persisted.

"Well, they'd never have made that at the sale," he told her. "Danny's beasts always fetch the worst prices in the township."

Liz felt as if someone had hit her hard. "Oh!" was all she could say. She sat looking down on the shore and the gulls. The waves were making a gentle whooshing sound as they came sideways one after the other onto the beach, but she was entirely taken up with what she had just heard. Hamish had made his remark so flatly that she felt sure he was telling the truth.

"Always make the worst prices!" she repeated mechanically as she tried to cope with the shattered picture of her father's competence. Hamish nodded. He was pitching small stones down the hill and listening to see whether he could hear them land. He wished he had held his tongue. He was sure old Hector had held his.

"How much do you think they would make at a sale?" Liz persisted, determined to know the worst.

"Och, I don't know," Hamish replied irritably, cross with himself. "It depends on trade. They might make £30 or a bit more—"

"Thirty pounds! Then Danny made £10 on each one?"

"Oh, I don't know how much, a bit anyway."

"Oh, what a horrid, beastly thing to do!" she cried out, suddenly angry. "And pretending all the time to be so friendly and sucking up to Dad and telling him it's great to have new ideas! I always knew it was all a sham!"

Hamish could not find it in his heart to condemn Danny quite so severely. If a man could make himself an extra £60 through taking advantage of a greenhorn, well, why shouldn't he?

"And he sits in our house and sits and sits!" she went on furiously, "and Mum and Dad think he's a great friend, when all he's doing is cheating them!"

Hamish cast about in his mind for something comforting to say. "He used to sit in your house a lot when your great-uncle had it, so perhaps it's just a habit he got into."

"Well, I wish he'd get out of it then. When Mum's in alone, he agrees with all the things she complains about, but if he's with Dad, he makes out the croft is wonderful!"

"What does he do when they're together?"

"Oh, then he makes a sort of noise which does for either!"

" 'Och aye, to be sure, to be sure!' " mimicked Hamish, and they both burst out laughing, which cheered Liz up.

"Of course he thought old Fergus was going to give him the croft," Hamish went on. "The old man'd say, 'You'll give me a hand with the stacking, lad, and I'll see you won't be the worse off!'—things like that, lifting tatties or turfing peat. Your uncle was awful hard, and he hated paying out cash. I expect he calculated he could get all the help he needed for nothing this way."

Liz could not like this way of behaving either. People ought not to promise things. "That was horrid, too!" she pronounced, but Hamish could not help thinking that if people let themselves be taken in, then it was largely their own fault, but he did not press this view on Liz, who was now looking very puzzled, indeed. She did not wish to feel the very least bit sympathetic toward Danny, but if what Hamish had told her was true, then he *had* been badly treated. "Goodness gracious!" she murmured to herself as all those new facts seethed together in her head, and then something else struck her—it was rather like suddenly seeing where a bit of jigsaw should go. "That's why she talked and talked about how handy the croft was with the road to the door, and then she gave me a look as if it was my fault and it didn't make sense to me—"

"Who are you talking about?" Hamish asked, quite lost.

"Mrs. Ross, Danny's wife. I went there with Dad, and I knew she didn't like me, and I couldn't think why. Of course, it's awful for them if the children can't go to school!"

Hamish went off into peals of laughter. "You are a muggins!" he explained when he could speak. "She doesn't care tuppence whether they go to school or not. When it's raining, she has a good excuse for lying in bed. If they did have your house, she'd soon be making a song and dance because the poor dears had to walk such a long way." He smiled at Liz, thinking that for a clever girl she was awfully green, forgetting that everything he knew so well was totally strange to her. Liz had the uncomfortable feeling that a situation which had looked perfectly simple was proving in reality to be very complex. Their father's decision to come and live in the country had affected others quite as much as themselves.

Hamish suddenly drew back and signaled to Liz to do likewise.

"Coo-ee!" came from below. "Coo-ee!" and an echo answered, "—ee!"

It came again. This time, "Hamish! Coo-ee! Where are you?" But Hamish stayed still till the sound had faded in the distance. Only then did he peer cautiously over the edge. Satisfied that Sandy was not in sight he slid out of the cave, beckoning Liz to follow. He went up, not down, following the narrowest of tracks.

"Do exactly as I do!" he ordered her, so she did just that, putting her hand in the holds he had used and her foot where he had put his. With her whole mind on the job, she did not look down or notice how far below the shore now was.

"Just this bit now!" said her guide as he crossed over some loose scree. Liz had time to notice how it fell away a few feet below where they were crawling across it. She hoped devoutly that they were over the worst and knew a rush of relief as they gained the close-cropped grass on the top of the cliff.

"Good!" commented Hamish when he had stopped panting. "I didn't want Sandy to find us in the hideout. Now you'll know a secret way up the cliff no one else does!" Liz

honestly felt she would have to be very hard pressed indeed before she used such a route, but Hamish went on. "Suppose the Norsemen were coming after you! They used to sail all down the coast, and people took their cattle inside duns and waited till they had gone. But this time you hadn't seen the smoke signal warning you their boats had been seen, and you were left outside all alone—"

"Oh, don't!" Liz begged him, disliking the bit about being the only one left outside. "Norsemen don't come here any more!"

Hamish grinned. "Well, then, it's Danny who's after you for taking his house! He's after you, taking huge strides, you haven't a hope unless you can gain this path, but he's got his arm out, he's got you by the ankle!" Liz shuddered, half in fun, half in earnest. Danny had very long arms and huge hands with knobbly knuckles—ugh! She jumped up and ran off by way of ending their talk. Hamish raced after her, overtook her, and was so delighted by his own speed that he forgot to tease her further.

8

Liz Is Rebuked

"Oh, has the plumber come at last?" Liz said, home from school to find the house in a turmoil.

"The plumber *and* the electrician! We waited weeks and weeks, and now they come on the same day."

"Oh good," cried Joan. "I'll wash my dollies' clothes on Saturday."

"And we can iron them, too," added Dorothy.

"That child!" exclaimed their mother, grabbing Nellie. "The times I've taken bits of wire out of her mouth today! Then they leave the back door open, and she's out in a jiffy. And as for your dad, of course there's no sign of him when he's needed—trust him for that. You look after her now, Liz, because I'm worn out." Liz began playing "This little pig went to market—" with her sister's toes. Dorothy and Joan ran upstairs and came back much excited to say the man was putting a tank up in the attic.

"Yes, a cistern," replied their mother wearily. "We're to have everything now. Dad says he'll put a bath in the corner of our bedroom and board it off, but where he thinks the money's to come from beats me. It's pay out and pay

out and nothing coming in, and there's only one end to
that!"

Liz had heard this complaint many times already, particularly when her mother was tired. Her father came in
full of bounce. "Bless my soul, Liz, now we really are
under way. Water and electricity! Send an invitation to
your sister Emily, love, as soon as we put in the bath.
What would you say to an immersion heater, eh?"

"What would I say to Buckingham Palace?" snapped
his wife.

"Look, Liz, your ma could do wi' a cuppa and so could
I, and Sam and Duggie and—"

"Old Uncle Tom Cobbley and all! I never saw such a
place for drinking tea all day. Why, you could float the
Queen Mary in it!"

"I'll make it, Dad," said Liz. "Come on, Nellie, poppet,
and help Liz get tea." The child staggered from cupboard
to table with butter and jam dishes held at crazy angles till
her father's nerve broke and he swept her up on his knee to
play "This is the way the ladies ride" to keep her out of
mischief.

When Liz had tea ready, Fred shouted at the foot of the
stair, "Hie there! Dugald! Danny! Tea!"

"Oh, not *him*," Liz muttered to her mother.

"Well, we don't have to pay him," she replied. Sammy
the electrician came in from outside, and they all sat down
together.

They were on to their second cups before Danny sidled
in. "Hey, what were you up to?" cried Fred. Liz noticed
that Danny's rough cheeks turned an even deeper shade of

red, and Fred said, "My, you're in a pickle! Better have a wash in the burn."

"I was—I was tidying things up a wee bit—yes, yes, just tidying up a wee bit," Danny told them before going out to wash.

"A lot of papers up there!" remarked Dugald.

"Now that's a fire risk," said Sam. "A garret full of papers and a faulty wire, and you've had it."

"You'd better clear all that junk out, then," said Fred.

His wife would have said it herself if he'd given her time, but now she bridled. "Tidy up that place indeed! Don't you think I've enough to do, four children to cook and wash for, let alone deal with the muck that comes in on your boots!" Danny overheard this last remark as he was coming in. He began scraping his boots on the worn mat till Mrs. Shearer told him impatiently to come on in, the kitchen was past praying for and his tea was getting cold. Danny drank his tea with a horrid sucking noise which got on Liz's nerves. It caused her to say to her father that evening when she had milked Rosie and he was leaning on the top bar of the pen admiring his stock, "They're not worth what you paid for them, Dad."

He swung round and stared at her. "Who told you that?"

"Hamish Macdonald—"

"Now, look here, Liz. The Macdonalds are all right in their own way and were kind when we came, but they fancy themselves, think they're the only ones to know the price of a beast—"

"Oh no, Dad! I'm sure they don't, but Hamish told me

Danny's cattle always make the worst price at the sale here—"

Her father became angry all of a sudden. "Do you mean to tell me you told that boy the price I paid for the stirks? Haven't you any more sense than that? How dare you tell him what I paid for them? That was a damn silly thing to do! Don't you know that nobody tells what he gives for a beast? It's time you learned a few things, my girl, outside your books!"

Liz stood dumb with astonishment. What on earth was the matter? Why in the world was her father so angry with her? All she wanted to do was to save him from making any more mistakes through believing in Danny, and when she thought of *him*, she became angry in her turn. "Danny's not a friend of yours," she said, her voice wobbling with agitation. "He wanted this croft for himself. Old Uncle Fergus told him he'd get it, so now he wants you to lose money—"

They stood facing each other like enemies in the gloom of the byre. Perhaps if Liz had left it at that, her words might have sunk in, but she wanted to make her case stronger and carried on, telling her father it had been a mistake to buy a cow that had already calved as they had lost the calf subsidy by so doing. (She had learned this from Old Anna.) But she was not allowed to finish. Her father took one step, seized her by the shoulders, and shook her till she gasped.

"Now, you understand this, my girl. You'll stop interfering in my affairs! Danny's been a good friend to me ever since we came—and I needed a friend. He's helped me buy a tractor, gi'en me a hand fencing and a help wi' draining, and I'm not going to listen to another word against him— do you understand that? And another thing, you'll be polite to him after this in *my* house. I dinna want any of your hoity-toity ways, my fine lady! Behave yersel' after this or I'll gi'e ye something ye won't forget in a hurry!"

He stepped back, and Liz fled from the byre, giving one small sob. In all her life her father had never spoken to her like that. How could telling him he had paid too much for six small stirks lead to such a terrible scene?

The next day was no better. He was in the house when they came home from school, and he pointedly ignored her. He asked Dorothy to go out with him to inspect the wonderful drains he had been making. Dorothy would much rather have stayed indoors, but she was sharp enough to realize that for once she was being put ahead of her sister, so off she went, hand in hand with her father, chatting merrily. Liz slipped out by the front and ran down the croft to a small copse of birch trees, plum colored in their winter bareness. Liz sat on a moss-covered rock and felt miserable among the pleasant-smelling trees. All day she had looked forward to coming home in the evening and making it up with her father. But now she realized that he was still angry with her and wished to punish her further. She longed to go to him and say, "I'm sorry, Dad. You were right, and I was wrong. I can see Danny is a good friend." But she couldn't. She had tried, she had said to herself that it was just possible that Danny really wished them well, but then all the evidence on the other side came up again—the price demanded for the stirks, the

buying of a cow that had already calved, the way he encouraged her mother to find everything difficult, the way
he praised her father to his face while making a fool of him
behind his back, the way he had let Angus off punishment.
"He is two-faced!" she exclaimed aloud, startling an old
ewe that had been busily grazing among the bushes. It
bounded off, reminding her of the night she had lost her
way and Hamish had rescued her, only she had not understood at the time how anxious he had been for her safety.
She smiled and sighed and wished she could talk to him,
but she must not do so any more since her father thought it
disloyal.

She sat subdued and silent through the evening meal.
Her father kept on talking about the draining he had done.
Liz remembered the Sunday evening on which Ian Macdonald had told them the life story of the liver fluke. With
a pang she heard her father say to Dorothy, "We'll beat
the liver fluke, Dotty. No more snails!"

Dorothy tossed back her pretty curls and made a face.
"Oh, Dad, don't talk about snails—they're horrid slimy
things!"

Fred cast a glance at Liz as if for understanding, but
she, looking down at her plate, missed it. He sighed. It
took him three days to find a way of making friends without loss of dignity.

On the third day the children found a large crate on the
porch. Liz said nothing, but Dorothy cried out, "Oh, is it
for me, Dad? Let me open it."

"It's for Liz," he replied. "You open it, Liz."

On hearing him use her name, Liz's heart rocketed up-

ward. She dropped on her knees beside the box. First she undid the rope and then with the aid of a claw hammer, which her father handed to her, she prized up the lid. There, sitting inside, was a roly-poly puppy, all black save for a white shirt front and one white paw. It looked up at Liz, putting its head on one side, cocking one ear and letting the other droop.

"Oh, Dad," she cried. "Is he for me? Oh, isn't he a darling?" She lifted the puppy in her arms and planted a kiss upon his head; then she kissed her father.

"There you are then!" said he, smiling, embarrassed but pleased with the success of his plan.

"Take him out of here!" ordered her mother. "No dogs in this house!"

"We'll find a place in the barn for him, Liz," her father said. Together they went over to the steading.

"We'll need to keep him frae the cow's feet till he learns sense," said her father. "We'll put a barricade across."

As he was looking for boxes, Looty came down from his favorite place on the hay, arching his back and mewing gently, but all of a sudden he became aware of the puppy, his hair rose, and he spat, retreated, and clawed his way up a beam.

"Oh, Looty, come down and be friends," Liz urged him.

"Better gi'e them time, Liz, as Hector was saying aboot the stirks. They canna make friends just in a minute."

When they had the puppy safely penned, they gave him bread and milk and watched him gulp them down.

"Thanks ever so much, Dad. I always wanted a dog."

"We'll need one," replied her father, and they smiled at one another, each determined that Danny Ruadh should not come between them again.

When the Easter holidays came, Liz had the time of her life looking after all the different animals. Rosie was now an old friend and milking no trouble at all. Old Anna had presented them with twelve newly-hatched chicks and their mother. "You see," she explained, "if I gave you a hen, she'd just come home again as the two houses are so close, but she'll stay with the chicks, and when they're big, I'll take the hen back." The children were all delighted with the chickens, Nellie especially. She longed to catch one of those yellow bundles of fluff, and many a battle she and the clucking hen fought over the issue. These engagements ended in defeat for Nellie, and she was found sitting howling as the hen marshaled her family to a safe distance.

The puppy was a continual fascination, growing so stout that his four little legs could barely support the superstructure. When in motion, he was apt to sit suddenly upon his tail, bowled over by his own weight. He grew also in moral sense and had a strong idea he should defend his own home. This led him to emit a series of shrill yaps that were immediately muted if the enemy was large. He often brought Liz's heart into her mouth by barking at Rosie as she came in at night, causing her to start and swerve, but she would find him under an upturned wheelbarrow uttering a few more squeaky defiances. Looty was still very standoffish and would scarcely come down for his saucer of milk.

Liz loved to watch her father plowing, while flocks of gulls screamed and called at the plow's tail, swooping for leather jackets and wire worms. In the birch copses the children found the first of the spring flowers, coltsfoot, daisies, and primroses. Catkins swung from the hazels and willows, while the birds sang from every tree.

One morning when she went to post letters, she found a tall, thin, dark young man behind the counter. She asked for two fourpenny stamps in a small voice. The young man leaned over the counter, putting a hand to his ear. She repeated her request more loudly, and Hamish, happening to be in the passage between the house and the office, heard her. "That you, Liz?" he asked, popping his head around the door. "Come on in!"

Ian was just making himself a pot of tea. "We are orphaned," he said, smiling at Liz. "Mum and Dad went off for the day. How are you? No more immersions in cold water?" Liz shook her head and was searching for something to say when the tall boy came in and helped himself to a cup from Ian's pot.

"I only made enough for myself," the latter objected. "You've had your breakfast!"

"Hours ago! I need another. 'Yoo should cultivate a spirit of giving!' " He pronounced this in a reedy voice, as if imitating someone.

"I'll give you something all right!" retorted Ian when his brother made to grab the last piece of toast, and fell upon him so that they rolled all over the kitchen floor in a tangle of arms and legs. The toast was in fragments by the time the battle was over. Ian smoothed back his hair with a laugh, and Murdo contented himself with a slice of bread.

"I'm astonished," said he between bites, "at your fighting in front of a lady." He bowed in Liz's direction.

"Lady? Where's the lady?" asked Hamish innocently, making his brothers laugh.

"Effect an introduction!"

"Oh, go on, you've met her already!" protested Hamish. His brother Murdo got on his nerves. Ian made the introduction, and Murdo bowed so low that a lock of black hair fell over his face.

"Ah!" he said. "I've heard all about you, the young lady who beats them all. Mind you, I always did think Hamish was a little wanting."

Liz did not like this criticism of her friend. "In that case," she said primly, "it would not be difficult to beat him."

Ian laughed. "Got you there, Murdo!"

"All the fault of the High School!" Murdo sighed, winding himself around a chair. "Now when I was with the Battle-Ax, I was as sharp as a needle."

"She's always talking about you and how good you were!" Liz blurted out, addressing Ian. Both brothers roared with laughter.

"You don't mean to say she never mentions Marvelous Murdo? I know what it is—she's muddling our names! 'Twas I she meant."

But Liz shook her head. "She only does it to make us feel small."

Hamish contributed, "I bet she didn't praise you when you were there!"

"Right first time, lad. There's hope for you yet."

"It must be wonderful to be at High School!" Liz ventured to say. This was greeted by another roar of laughter. "Abandon hope all ye that enter here!" said Murdo. It was clear that no one in the Macdonald household agreed with Liz's romantic notions about learning.

Hamish and Liz went off exploring that morning, the first of several. They followed the course of the Gask stream, slithering down the steep banks, grabbing branches and roots to keep from falling. Down in the bed of the stream, they clambered over slippery rocks, digging their fingers and toes into tiny niches, their faces and hands soaked by spray. Hamish spotted a nest, but Liz had trouble seeing it even when it was pointed out. "Use your eyes!" Hamish adjured her. He was putting his new companion through her paces. Could she climb wet, slippery rocks as well as she had climbed the sea cliff? Would she

make a fuss about the cold spray? Would she make a fuss
if she fell in? Yes, indeed she would. Having overbalanced
on a shaky stone, she was tipped into the icy water and
came out gasping. "Oh, oh, oh! I'm off home—I'm soaking."

"A boy wouldn't mind," Hamish said.

"Well, I'm not a boy, and I do!" retorted Liz, and she
took to her heels, damaging her reputation with Hamish,
but after all he had known perfectly well that a girl, however good she was, could never come up to a boy's stand-
ards.

Liz didn't care about that, but she much disliked her
wet hair flapping against her back. "Mum," she said, "I'll
get Hector to cut my hair." Her mother did not think the
old man would make a good job of it. Liz told her he cut
everyone's hair.

"Oh, well! I suppose it doesn't matter very much. Your
hair is not pretty like Dorothy's," her mother said, and Liz
took this for permission. In the evening she ran up to Hector's cottage, where she received a warm welcome, not un-
mixed with reproaches because of her long absence.

"I know," said Liz. "I'm sorry, but I'm always out all
day. Oh, it's lovely! Hamish took me up the Gask burn,
climbing up beside the wee waterfalls, and he found a
blackbird's nest this morning."

Hector shook his head. "Don't be letting him take you
into these wild places! I've seen that lad climb a cliff a goat
would have steered clear of! I have with my own eyes.
'That's tempting providence,' I told him. He didn't know I
was there. 'If you were saving a man's life, that would be

all right, but to put yourself in danger for no reason, that's foolhardy!' I said."

"He's a nice lad," commented old Anna, knitting by the window, "and a good worker." Hector ruminated over this opinion, turning his empty pipe in his hands. "Oh, aye," he acknowledged presently. "He can work all right, but then he breaks out like a young horse running away with a cart."

Liz explained what she wanted. The old lady raised her hands in protest. "Cut off all that beautiful hair! When we were young, we wanted to have hair so long we could sit on it!"

"I expect you had pretty hair," Liz replied, "but mine's long and straight and such a dull color."

Hector picked up a tress in his hands to examine it. "It's very pretty hair," he said, "fine and soft and not plain brown either. There's glints of red and gold in it." These opinions quite astonished Liz, who had always believed her hair to be dull. They almost made her change her mind till she remembered tumbling in the stream and the time it took to dry. Seeing her determined, Hector placed her in a chair, wrapped her in a clean towel, and put his scissors to work. When it was all over, Liz gave her head a shake and enjoyed the feeling of lightness. She was sure she would be better able to follow Hamish now.

But after she had gone, the old man took one of the locks and curled it around his finger and then placed it in his waistcoat pocket. That woman (by this he meant Liz's mother), that woman didn't know a good thing when she saw one.

Hamish hardly noticed the difference except to say it would be handier, but the boys back at school looked at her in surprise. Why, she was very near to being a boy herself! During recess they sat on the playground wall considering the matter.

"She's like one of ourselves now," pronounced Alec John. Angus hoped someone would disagree, but the rest murmured their agreement. "She's not 'big' on it (by which he meant conceited), so why should we bother about beating her any more?"

Jim and Ian agreed heartily. "It's summertime—we'll be after the sheep," said Jim. "Maybe you could study yourself, Hamish, and beat her?"

Hamish let it be understood that it would be the easiest thing in the world, but on the whole he agreed with the rest. "There's no one could stay indoors on a fine summer's evening learning spellings."

No one disputed this. Book learning in winter was just tolerable, but in summer it was out of the question.

It was in this way that Liz found herself in undisputed possession of the top place in the class.

9

Sheep Gathering

Liz, coming home from school one afternoon, heard Hamish shouting and waited for him to catch up. He was swinging his satchel in the best of spirits. "I'm going gathering tomorrow!" he announced.

"Gathering what?" Liz asked. It seemed to her a reasonable question, but he stared at her in disbelief. Not know what gathering meant? She must be kidding!

"Gathering sheep, of course!"

"Oh! Why?"

"It's the first gathering of the year, and it's to find how many lambs there are altogether and to mark them. Look, Liz, Dad's got lumbago and he can't gather tomorrow, so he says I'm to go in his place. You'd better come with me."

"Me!" exclaimed Liz in astonishment. "I don't know how to gather sheep. Anyway, I'll be in school."

"Oh, school be blowed! Gathering is more important. No, but I'll tell you why I want you to come. Dad was saying perhaps he'd better ask Angus because he's quite good with a dog, and I said I'd do it just as well, only it's a bit of a job alone because while you're making sure you're not missing any down on the shore, the others can double back. I don't want to make a mess of it and have Dad saying he should have gotten Angus."

Liz readily sympathized with this argument. "OK, I'll come, but you'll have to explain properly what you want me to do."

"Good! That's fine. Yes, I'll explain it all tomorrow. Meet me at Calum Mor's byre at seven and don't be late."

Liz was up in plenty of time, but Billy, the puppy, caused delay by crawling out of the byre and dashing up to her in an ecstasy at seeing her out so early, wagging his tail so hard that it nearly went into his mouth. She had to harden her heart and put him back inside, tying him this time. "I'll take you next year when you have sense," she promised him, but his high, piercing yaps and heartrending wails followed her far along the road. Outside Calum's byre Hamish was waiting.

"You're late!" was his greeting before she had time to explain. He had Lassie, a black-and-white bitch, with him, but he was to keep her to heel as she was young and might take advantage of him if sent far. She now jumped up on Liz, whining and licking her hands in welcome.

"It's a lovely morning," said Liz, looking around at the loch, still as a sheet of glass.

Hamish nodded. "Be bright later," he prophesied, "but come on or we'll be late." This was nonsense as they had a bare two miles to cover, while the men at the far end of the loch had to go twice the distance, but Hamish's responsibilities were weighing heavily upon him. Once out on the common grazing, he explained to Liz what he wanted her to do. "You go down to the shore, at least not quite down. Keep along the top above the shore and keep looking down into all the wee coves and bays and whistle if you see sheep in them. They'll run out when they hear you. All you've got to do is to follow behind. Don't worry if they run uphill because that's where I'll be, and I'll turn them, but whatever you do, don't let them run back, for we'll lose them if you do."

So they separated, Hamish keeping on straight and Liz making down for the shore. She had often taken walks in this direction but had not realized how irregular the coast was till she had to inspect each tiny cove and inlet. Some were empty, only a solitary cormorant flying out, disturbed by her shouts. In others she found small numbers of ewes with their lambs. These were dazzling white in their curly coats, in striking contrast to their mothers' dark fleeces, matted and tangled bits of wool trailing down like draggled tail sluts. To begin with, everything went according to plan. The sheep ran out, scampering up the steep slopes, and the lambs bleated after them. As soon as they stopped, the lambs rushed in to suckle, drawing both milk and comfort at the one time. The sight of their tails waggling from side to side made Liz smile, but being out on business, she had to shout loudly, "Way wide!" as she advanced upon them, pretending she was addressing a dog. This deceived the sheep, and they made off at a rapid trot, following the narrow paths their own hoofs had made up the grassy banks, disappearing in single file over the top.

Liz hurried after, enjoying the chase. Pigeons coming out of a cave below startled her once with the clap and whir of their wings, and duck, which had been swimming close in shore in the early morning calm, flew out to sea. Things were going splendidly, and Hamish and she would make a clean sweep of the low ground.

In the next cove was a ewe with a lamb. Liz shouted as usual, but the ewe, although it raised its head and looked at her, resumed grazing. The girl tried again, waving her arms and using every expression she had ever heard Hector use to his bitch, Fancy, but it made no difference. This ewe went on feeding as if it were alone in the landscape. There was nothing for it but to climb down and drive the beast out. She slithered down the green slope till she was face to face with it, whereupon it stamped its foot while its lamb ran in to suckle. Hamish had said nothing about sheep defying orders to move.

"Way off!" she cried. "Shoo!" She was delighted to see it climb the bank and hurried after it only to find that it had run back instead of joining the rest. Oh dear, this was a setback, and just when she had been doing so well! However, as Hamish had said not to let them run back, she must go after this one. Using cunning, she circled around the ewe and began to close in on it. Drawing near once more, she shouted again to her imaginary dog. The beast lifted its head, looking at her from its slit yellow eyes. "Shoo-shoo—!" Liz yelled, dancing and waving her arms. Obligingly the ewe trotted off in the right direction. Liz felt her heart swell with pride. She'd been one too many for it. Even without a dog, she had turned it! Hamish and Angus both had dogs, but she, Liz— At this point in her triumph, the ewe turned once more and galloped right past

her in spite of all the waving and yelling she could do. With hate in her heart, Liz went through the whole performance twice more. "If you do that again, you'll be sorry!" she told the ewe. "You'll be very sorry!" But even to her own ears the threat sounded thin. The second time around, when the ewe had trotted quietly fifty yards in the right direction and then bolted, Liz sat down, near to weeping with rage and vexation. The horrid beast seemed to take pleasure in making a fool of her. What could she do now? She had lost sight of the rest, the ones she had gathered first. Should she not go after them, for even if she once more pursued the ewe, she could not make her come. While she sat in this state of indecision, a small breeze blew up, ruffling the still water and cooling her hot cheeks. Shouts came from above, and looking up, she saw Hamish. She jumped to her feet and started trying to explain what had happened, but shout as she might, he was too far off to hear her. He came running down, and she went running up and burst out all about the ewe and how she had done everything she could, but it had defeated her. Liz had expected reproaches and references to Angus, but all Hamish did was to shrug and say, "Oh, that one! You should just have left her. Even the dogs can't manage her!"

Liz's temper boiled up. "Do you mean to say," she demanded, "that you knew about this one and you didn't tell me? How was I to know I was to leave her? You *said* to bring *every* sheep!" Her voice quivered with indignation, but Hamish thought she was going to cry.

"Oh, good life!" he said hastily. "It doesn't matter. Come on or we'll be late. Goodness knows where the rest have gotten to."

"I couldn't care less!" Liz shouted furiously after him. He hadn't even the decency to say he was sorry, after making her run and run—it really was too bad, and she had a good mind to go home and leave him there, him and his stupid sheep. She never wanted to see a sheep again!

But when she had cooled down a little, going home seemed dull, so presently she followed on and caught up with the flock, what she had gathered and what he had gathered now mingling in one bleating, baaing mass. Lassie wove swiftly from side to side, keeping all in their places with an occasional short, sharp yap. The turf was soft under foot, the sky blue above, and suddenly Liz burst out laughing. It was such fun to be out in the early morning that she felt like leaping and skipping like the lambs for joy. Hamish shot her a glance and grinned, glad to see that she had recovered. Now they could see the gray stone walls of the old fank looming ahead.

"We'll take it easy," he said. "They'll go inside better that way." When they drew nearer, they saw two men already waiting at the far side of the big gate, and they held a split-up wool bag between them to prevent the sheep escaping on that side. The leading ewe gave them a look and turned quietly in at the big gate, the rest trotting after her. Calum Mor and Sandy Lockhart dragged over the wooden gate and fixed it securely, leaning over it when that was done to examine the condition and number of the lambs and to decide whether they were equal to last year's crop or better. Hamish went around the side of the fank and seated himself on the wall. It was quite low on the outside, but there was a six-foot drop on the inside, making it impossible for the sheep to jump out. Liz joined him, glad to rest after all the running she had done. Hamish kept scanning the hillside above and along the loch side, but they heard the advancing flock before they saw it. Faint bleats and fainter barks came down the breeze, and then there was a sudden rush of sheep foaming down between two lines of rock. They looked like a stream in spate when the water charges down after several days of rain. Liz's eye was caught by movement further to the right, and she saw some sheep break away and make a dash for freedom.

"They're going to get away!" she cried.

"So they are!" Hamish exclaimed, but even as he spoke, they saw the rush come to a sudden halt. At first the children could not make out what had halted them. No one was ahead of them, no one had shouted, but as they watched the fugitives scampering back to the main body, they made out a black-and-white collie close on their heels, controlling the whole band with effortless ease.

"Oh, what a clever dog!" Liz exclaimed.

"It's Danny's dog, Moss," Hamish told her. "He's a topper! He's done all that by himself." The flock, reunited, came running downhill in an uproar of baaing and barking, with the high bleats of the lambs sounding extraordinarily sad, as if they were expressing the bewilderment of all lost creatures. Hamish jumped down and went to join the men at the gate on the down side of the fank—sheep try always to run uphill. Now the cries of the men increased the general commotion as they closed in on the flock, waving their long crooks and shouting, "Sho! Ho! Ho!" The collies wove back and forth, pouncing on any ewe bold enough to attempt escape. This flock coming down from the high hills and the cliffs was wilder than the first, and it took men and dogs some time to pen them safely in the fank, but at last they were all in and the gate barricaded as before. The tumult died slowly away, although the dogs could not be at once convinced that their services were no longer needed and kept jumping on and off the fank wall, eyeing the flock and giving vent to sharp yaps till their masters told them sharply to, "Clap down, will you? Clap!"

Liz and Hamish had gone back to the wall, and Angus joined them. He had been out with his father right to the far end of their farm and was inclined to boast. Hamish, wishing to keep his end up, said that he and Liz had taken every sheep off the low ground except, of course, the old ewe. He laughed and explained how Liz had nearly had heart failure trying to bring her in. The men who were now standing near heard his story.

"Well, you were hardy to try and turn her!" commented Donald, one of the shepherds. "She's not canny, that one! If I've time in the evening, I'll take a turn along the shore and catch the lamb. I see you got the most of them," he went on, casting a keen eye over the flock. "See that one, Calum—she's brought her lamb in with her this year. Mind she lost a grand lamb to the fox last year, and the year before her lamb went over the cliff so it was about time she was keeping one alive."

Liz marveled to hear him. How could he possibly know one sheep from another, she said to Hamish. Why ever not, he replied. She did not mistake him for Sandy, and he did not mistake her for Dorothy. Liz did not think this a fair comparison. She was bigger than Dorothy, but the sheep were all about the same size. Donald, who had now seated himself with his back to the fank wall and his face to the sun, smiled a slow smile that lit up his craggy features. "You'll not forget that old ewe! You'll know her the next time you see her!"

They laughed in a kindly fashion and praised her, saying she would make a good shepherd some day, making Liz feel like a heroine. Reflecting on what Donald had said, she recognized its truth. She would know that ewe again, she hated her so much.

Everyone was now taking sandwiches and flasks of tea from their knapsacks. When they saw that Liz had nothing, they shared their food with her, and Hamish gave her a cup of tea from his flask. Liz, sitting warm in the sun, the green grass all around and the sea rolling blue to the horizon, felt she had never enjoyed a picnic so much.

Presently more men arrived, her father among them, and shortly afterward work began. Liz, perched on the wall, watched men go into the big fank and separate a small cut of sheep. These they drove through a gate in the top corner of the fank into a smaller fank just below where she sat. This small fank had four gates leading into yet other enclosures. Hamish explained that the one below them was the catching fank. But why, Liz wondered, were some sheep put into one pen and some into another. Hamish again explained that hoggs, the year-old sheep, wedders, the two-year-olds, and rams were all put into one fank that day and nothing done to them, but the milk ewes were put into the back fank to wait till the lambs rejoined them after being marked.

There was a man at each gate ready to swing it open when another man came along with a sheep. Liz saw her father standing at the gate of the back fank. He gave her a wave, saying, "Here's me doorman at the Ritz!" It was a scene of apparent confusion, but a pattern presently emerged with each man playing his part. Down below her were Danny Ruadh and Calum Ban. They were dealing with the rams. But all at once everything came to a halt. There had been a hitch somewhere.

"What is it?" Liz asked Hamish.

"Sheep got into the wrong fank, I expect," he told her. Men were talking loudly in a group near her father, and then she saw Donald Mor come out of the back fank, dragging a wedder between his knees.

"Sorry, folk," said Fred, whose fault it had been, for he had opened the gate to the wrong animal. "Have to learn ma trade!" Donald and Sandy accepted his apology with a good grace, saying it was easy to make mistakes, but Danny and Calum muttered together. Liz picked out a Gaelic word here and there that she had learned at school—"*Gallda*," a lowlander, and "*anns an rathad*," in the way.

Liz blushed and felt uncomfortable, for she feared they meant that her father was in the way. It was very unfair of them to say so because he was doing his level best to help. Calum and Danny went on muttering together till Calum, happening to look up, caught her eye and fell abruptly silent. This confirmed her suspicions. Somehow the day did not seem so bright after that. She moved farther along the wall out of earshot of Danny and his friends. Hamish had gone off on an errand, and she was alone when Donald called up to her to go to the well. "The pail is lying beside my knapsack," he said, "and the well is over beyond the yellow flags."

Liz ran off, glad of something to do, and found the well, but it was choked with watercress, not having been used that summer. She dipped her hand into the ice-cold water and pulled the weed out, clinging in long green strands to her fingers. It was easy to clean off the weed, but it took time for the water to clear. While waiting, she made a little channel for the overflow and admired the yellow flags. At last she filled her pail and ran back, thinking Donald would have become impatient. When she reached the wall, she saw Danny holding a big ram. He sat astride it, his hands gripping the huge curled horns. Even as she looked, Danny lost his grip, and the beast plunged forward

down the length of the fank. Fred, the only man free at the
moment, grabbed the ram's horn but was swung off his
feet as the animal charged past. In spite of this he clung
on, with the result that he was rammed against the wall.
Donald Mor dropped the lamb he was holding, flung his
leg over the ram, and grasped both horns.

"Let go!" he shouted to Fred. "Let go! I've got him."
Fred let go and picked himself up, rubbing the back of his
head and his shoulders.

"Best keep out of a ram's way unless you're sure you can
hold him," said Donald as he dragged the brute back to
the gate it should have gone in at.

At this moment Liz pointed suddenly at Danny and
said, loudly and clearly, "He let it go! He let it go! He
meant to!"

It was like shouting aloud in church. There was an ap-
palled silence. Everyone stayed fixed in the posture her
words had caught him in. Then Danny broke into a babble
of denials. The beast had gotten away from him—why
would he let it go? What was the sense in that?

Everyone now joined in. "Losing your grip, Danny?"
asked Donald, with a trace of irony.

Her father shouted angrily to Liz to belt up if she
couldn't talk sense. Of course Danny was not to blame.
Next time he'd hold the brute, see if he didn't.

Sandy Lockhart praised Fred's courage in grabbing the
ram. Rams were not to be treated lightly. He could tell
many a tale about rams.

The accident, if accident it was, released feelings running usually well below the surface. Now they bubbled up

to the top. Why should Glasgow people get good crofts when they didn't know the first thing about stock and were as much use as a bairn in the fank? What they needed was a tenant who knew his way among sheep and could be a real help. Ever since Hector and Old Fergus had grown too old for such work, they had been short-handed. Calum, William Archie, and Danny grumbled in some such terms, while Sandy, Donald Mor, and one or two others said the man had been left the croft and had a perfect right to take it and was proving himself a willing worker. He'd learn. The talk died away as the pressure of work took over. Liz had not been able to follow the arguments, but she could feel the tension. The pleasant, friendly companionship of the morning had vanished. Her father could say what he liked—she knew Danny had meant to hurt him. In her mind's eye she could see his hands letting go. No one else would have seen him, being busy, but she had arrived back at the wall at that very minute. Oh, what had she done with the pail of water? She had forgotten all about it! She delivered it to Donald, who thanked her kindly. That was one of the best wells on their hill, he said, and, having drunk, handed the pail on to the next man.

Shortly afterward the schoolboys came rushing to join them. The Battle-Ax was flaming mad because three of them had skipped school. She was thinking up awful punishments for the morning, Ian said. "Who cares?" retorted Hamish. That was for another day. He lived in the moment, and the moment was good.

10

The Intruder

The school worked itself up into a ferment of excitement over the "Mod," the Gaelic festival of song and story, held in June. Children carried home some of the excitement with them. Mrs. Shearer had been busy for weeks making kilts for Dorothy and Joan, both in the choir. At last the kilts of Mackay tartan were ready for trying on. Their mother was on her knees giving a pull here and a tug there, making the girls turn slowly to see if the kilts hung properly, when their father came in and, seeing what was forward, raised his arms over his head and crying "Heuch!" danced the first steps of the Highland Fling. The girls burst out laughing, but their mother told him to stop that nonsense, for Joan's kilt was hanging down at the back and she was restless.

"It's hanging grand," he exclaimed, "just like a dead man from the gallows!"

"Now, Fred!"

"Well! Well! What about ye and me gaeing tae the Mod tomorrow, Gracie? Are ye on?"

His wife, who was just putting a pin in a pleat, stopped

and stared at him. "You and me? What would happen to Nellie?"

"Nellie'd be as good as gold, eh, poppet?" and he swung the little girl up to the ceiling to her intense delight. Put back on the floor, she kept shaking her dark curls, saying over and over, "Nellie good go'd, Nellie good go'd," making her sisters laugh, but her mother shook her head and went on with her pinning.

"She'd be good for five minutes, and then she'd start crying or talking or both, and I'd have to take her out, so I'd rather not go at all than that."

But her husband did not give up. "Tell ye what, Gracie. We'll leave Lizzie in charge of Nellie, and you and me'll take a day off! When did we have a day off last?"

"Looking for the plumber," replied his wife as she made Joan turn around.

"Yon was nae a day off, woman! Yon was business! What aboot it, Liz? Could ye manage the wean?"

Liz had not been going to the Mod. She was no singer, but she and Hamish had planned to go exploring further afield than they had yet reached. If she had to look after Nellie, they could not go. But she had seen her mother's face light up, so she managed to nod. "I'll manage OK, Dad."

"Good girl!" cried her father, clinching the matter, "and the next time there's an outing, you'll be the first to go."

"I'll see Portree before Liz!" piped up Dorothy, giving a skip and a hop.

"Now, Miss Cheeky, less o' it. Yer sister will be at the High School."

"Well, I don't want to go there!" said Dorothy, pouting. "I'm going to be top of the pops!"

"Well, jist tell me when ye're to be on and I'll turn television off. I canny stand yon squawking!"

"I don't squawk, Dad, I sing," replied Dorothy with dignity, "and Miss Fergusson thinks I'll win the Silver Medal!"

By nine o'clock the following morning they had gone.

"Mum away!" Nellie murmured over and over. "Mum away!"

"Wheest, Nellie, love. Mum won't be long, and here's Liz to look after you. We'll go and feed the hens." So she mixed the hens' mash and carried it out, Nellie trotting behind.

"Chook, chook, chook!" they called together, and the hens came scampering, all fifteen. Then they had to go and feed the hen with the chickens. The hen still lifted little bits in her beak and clucked to the chickens to come, but they were big now and needed no encouragement to gobble up every crumb. Unnoticed by Liz, Nellie helped herself to a mouthful of mash.

"Who's a bad girl?" came a voice behind them, and they turned to see Hamish shaking his head at Nellie. She swallowed the mouthful in such haste she almost choked. Hamish hoisted her up onto his shoulders and ran around, with her laughing and slapping his head.

"Oh, Hamish!" said Liz dolefully. "I can't come out— I've to look after Nellie."

Hamish frowned and looked thoughtful. "Um, have

you?" he murmured. "We could take her to the shore, I suppose—no, tell you what, Mum will look after her! We've no visitors in today and everyone else is away, so that's all right." The Macdonalds kept tourists.

Liz raked out the fire, closed the door, and ran after Hamish who had gone ahead with Nellie. He and the little girl had been good friends for some time now, and Nellie used to look out for him on his way back from school. Hamish's mother agreed to look after Nellie, and the two youngsters slipped off.

"Oh, this is lovely!" said Liz. "Let's go right to the top of Ben Mor." But Hamish shook his head. He had another idea.

"I've something great to show you!" he announced. "You follow me!"

He took the way they had gone in the Easter holidays. The trees had been bare then but were now wearing their freshest green. Some of the young bracken stalks had uncurled, but others still made croquet hoops. Ferns were growing tall, white clover scented the grass, larks were in full chorus, and the blackbird piped his sweet ditty by the bank of the stream. They clambered down as they had done before and came to the rock-encircled pool.

"There!" said Hamish, triumphantly pointing. Liz looked and looked, but all she could see was an old tub floating in the water, a round wooden tub with two handles, not an object to arouse feelings of joy. Hamish, however, was full of his own cleverness. "I got her up here all by myself," he boasted. "I rolled her wherever I could, and where I couldn't, I carried her and she was some weight."

"I suppose so!" agreed Liz politely. At this point he became aware of a lack of enthusiasm.

"Don't you see?" he said impatiently. "She's our boat!"

"Our boat?"

"Just you wait and see this!" He kicked off his shoes, pulled off his socks, rolled his jeans above his knees, and waded into the pool at the shallow end. Getting a grip on the tub, he pulled it alongside the flat rock on which Liz stood. "Now she's at the quay! Watch me go aboard!" Gingerly he put first one foot in—when the tub dipped toward him—and then the other. "Ticklish operation, that!" he commented, grinning at Liz. "Get me a stick till I navigate the *Queen Mary* to the far side."

"*Queen Mary?* Her? More like *Saucy Sal*," replied Liz, who was not yet sold on this craft and still longed to climb the high hill.

Hamish pushed her carefully off. "I know what to call

her," he shouted back at Liz. "The *Queen Elizabeth*—
that's her name, of course!"

As at this moment the tub, being caught in a current,
began to turn like a top, Liz could afford to laugh scorn-
fully. "You can't do anything but turn like a top!" she
mocked. Put on his mettle, Hamish gave one push too
many, and the tub tipped him neatly into the pool.

Liz roared with laughter. "Oh, you do look funny! Oh,
you're no use at all. Let me try!"

"Do!" said Hamish cordially as he climbed up on the
rock, dripping water like a fountain. Liz stepped cheerfully into the tub, much too cheerfully, for it at once unbal-
anced and tipped her out. It was now Hamish's turn to
laugh.

"You didn't even sit in her!" he said, choking. "You
didn't stay one minute."

Liz was soaking and crestfallen. She had imagined she
could sail the odd craft. Now she knew better and determined to master the art even if it took all day. It did take
several more duckings (like a Halloween apple) before
she succeeded in staying in it as it bobbed against the rock
barrier, but she could not do what Hamish did and cross to
the other side. He passed under the little waterfall.
"Lovely!" he shouted as the spray covered him.

They giggled and mocked at each other's efforts till
their sides ached. Billy, the puppy, who had trailed them
to the pool, having eaten through his rope, sat on the bank
howling because he was convinced his beloved mistress
was drowning. Hamish swore he'd drown *him* if he did not
dry up.

The sunshine filtered down to them through a screen of hazel and birch leaves and gleamed on pancakes of white foam, making the little waterfall sparkle like a diamond necklace. At last, tired out, the children sat on the rock and let the tub drift off under the boughs.

"Gosh! I'm hungry!" exclaimed Hamish. "It must be dinnertime."

"I'd better go home and get dry clothes," said Liz, suddenly aware of how wet she was.

"Oh, Mum will give you clothes," asserted Hamish. "Come on! I'm starving."

Liz ran, panting after him, thinking she was always turning up on the Macdonalds' doorstep either wet or cold or both. However, by the time they reached the post office, their thin clothes were almost dry, so they decided to say nothing of what they had been doing.

Hamish's mother had put dinner into the oven when they did not turn up and now served them a mutton stew full of vegetables. This was followed by semolina pudding and stewed rhubarb, and they finished off with a cup of tea and a chunk of shortcake.

"Oh, I won't be able to eat another bite today!" declared Liz.

Hamish scoffed at so mean a capacity, and his mother was sure she'd be hungry long before her family got home.

"I wonder how they're doing! Miss Fergusson promised to give me a ring if she won the shield for the best small school choir."

"Who cares!" remarked Hamish, helping himself to another bit of shortcake. "Think of sitting in a stuffy hall on a day like this, listening to the same song sung over and over again. Drive you up the wall! Everyone in a kilt, and tartan curtains hanging all over the place."

Liz thought privately that it might be rather fun. His mother said all the children looked very nice in their kilts and white blouses, and she liked to hear them.

"Perhaps your Dorothy will win some of the competitions! I'm sure she has a very sweet voice."

"Sweet as a crow!" Hamish muttered. Nellie, meantime, was fast asleep on the sofa, a picture of innocence, having spent the morning getting into cupboards, where she had no business to be.

The telephone rang in the post office. Peigi Mhoir came back to say there was a telegram for the other end of the township. Hamish would have to go.

"Always the way!" he grumbled. "Can't ever get a day off! I was going swimming."

"Well, we had a lovely morning," said Liz. She dried the dishes, remembering the night when she had been too shy to leave her seat. Peigi Mhoir was also remembering the Shearers' arrival.

"Are you missing the town now, or would you be sorry if you had to go back?" she said.

"Oh, I don't want to go back *now!*" Liz replied instantly, surprising herself by her own certainty. She had wanted to go back for so long that she had taken it for granted she still did till asked.

When, she wondered, had she changed her mind?

"Och well, it was a great change for you!" Peigi Mhoir went on in her comfortable way. "And you came at a bad time in the winter, and one of the worst winters we've had for years."

"Yes, I was always cold," Liz said, and yet on her way home, trying to recollect these days exactly, she found she could not—how she had walked this selfsame path, head down against the blizzard, ears tingling, hands swollen with cold. And how bleak it had all looked! A waste of gray sea and sky and dull brown moorland. Now it was glowing with color: the grass a green counterpane spangled with yellow, white, and blue wild flowers, sea and sky blue, and the distant hills a dimmer, distant blue. She sat for a minute to let Nellie rest, and all around bees hummed, exploring the clover, bluebottles buzzed, and a fly took the chance to bite her bare arm. Ouch! She smacked at it, and it flew off. Nellie and she wandered slowly homeward. In the house the child went from room to room, saying, "Mam? Mam?" and then "Mam gone! Mam gone!" till Liz felt quite melancholy.

"Mam will be back soon!" she told Nellie. "Nellie, run out and play while Liz sweeps the kitchen." However, when she had tidied up and washed all the dishes, she had to take Nellie in as she was going to make the beds. The child climbed the stairs slowly, putting the right foot first each time. "Up-a-tair! Up-a-tair!" she chanted. They made the big bed together, playing peekaboo around the end, laughing a good deal. But in a silence, as Liz was straightening the candlewick quilt, she heard a noise overhead. She paused to listen, but there was no sound. It could have been something from outside, a bird perhaps on the roof. Seagulls and jackdaws often perched there. Yes, that's what it must have been, she reckoned. Their feet would make that sort of scuffling noise on the slates. She bent to put her mother's nightgown under the pillow and heard the noise again, a shuffling, coming from the attic. But who could be in the attic? Burglars were commonplace in Glasgow but not in the island. Why, people often went out without locking their doors, and that reminded her she had gone out that morning and left the doors unlocked all day. No, no, it was more likely to be rats than human beings. Yet as she stood straining her ears, she became certain that someone was moving with the utmost stealth above her. Gently she moved toward the door and was putting her hand on the knob when Nellie, tired of being ignored, shouted peekaboo from the far side of the bed. Then everything happened at once. There was a thud just outside and the clatter of boots going down the stairs. Liz threw open the door, crying, "Who's there?" but the boots had reached the downstairs hall. Liz dashed down, not thinking what she would do supposing the intruder were to stand his ground, but the kitchen door was open and she heard the scraping noise the back door made as it was dragged back. When she reached it, the man was already out of sight, but if she could reach the corner of the house, she would see him where the road ran straight for fifty yards. She'd see him all right and then she'd know. The next moment she was flat on her face in the path, the wind knocked out of her. She lay groaning, tears coursing down her cheeks from the shock and disappointment. Something warm and wet was licking her face and whining. Billy! Why, of course, that was it. She hadn't tripped over something cleverly left by the fugitive—she had tripped over Billy! And the thief had made good his escape! She sat up dizzy and sick, her forehead aching, and the puppy threw himself in an ecstasy across her knees. "Oh, Billy," she reproached him tearfully. "How could you be so silly? Why didn't you trip *him* up? You're real stupid—that's what you are." And she sat feeling very sorry for herself while tears and blood trickled down her face.

Howls came from the house behind her. Nellie! She must have fallen downstairs. Liz struggled to her feet, her own pains forgotten in this new disaster. Even as she ran, she pictured Nellie lying dead and her mother accusing her of her sister's death. But there was no corpse at the foot of the stair, and the noise coming from above was reassuring. There, sure enough, on the top step sat Nellie, mouth wide open, ready for the next terrific bellow.

"Oh, Nellie," her sister cried thankfully. "Wheest, pet, don't cry. Liz is here. Liz won't leave you." But Nellie could not stop crying. Liz picked her up and carried her downstairs and held her on her knee in the big armchair, rocking her to and fro, till at last she quieted down. They sat thus for a long time, while Liz's head ached more and more painfully. What could she do? There was Nellie, and there was the cow to bring home and the hens to feed and the fire to light again for the family's coming home, and she felt so sick that she did not see how she could cope. "I'll go to Hector's," she thought. "Anna will look after us, and Hector will bring home Rosie with his own cows." Yes, that was what she would do. But when she rose, Nellie began to whimper. She wanted her mother and was now cross and fretful. "We'll go to Hector's," Liz said.

"Nellie walk!" But Nellie wouldn't. She clung to Liz and began to wail, "Mam, Mam, Mam." Liz picked her up in her arms and carried her out of the house. Once again the dog dashed at them in delight.

"Oh, stop it, Billy!" said Liz crossly, feeling she might fall at any moment. The little procession climbed the steep brae to Hector's cottage. "Oh," thought Liz, "once I'm inside, it'll be all right. They'll look after me!" She turned the doorknob, but it would not open. She turned it again and again, knocked on the door, and banged, but it was all useless. The house was empty, and it was then she remembered that it was Anna's day to go to Broadford for the physiotherapist, and Hector for once must have gone with her. Liz sank down on the doorstep while tears forced themselves through her closed eyelids and down her cheeks. She felt very sick, and it would be hours before her parents came. She wiped her eyes and attempted to look all around. There was no one to be seen, no smoke even from distant houses as the township had taken the day off and gone to the Mod.

Somehow she got back home, went inside, locked the door, and bolted all the windows, and it was only when she had finished that she became afraid the thief might have come in again when they were out. She stood and listened, then gave herself a shake. Of course there was no one inside! He had been running fast and was miles away by now. When she had washed her face, gingerly wiping off the blood, she made supper for Nellie and then managed to get her to bed. Downstairs once more, she thought of making herself a meal, but a wave of nausea went over her, and she had to lie down. Still she kept listening, although her

common sense told her there was no need. Billy whined at
the back door.

She opened the door, and he came bounding up as usual
but refused to come inside, slipping away from Liz's out-
stretched hand. He sat a little distance off, head on one
side, wagging his tail. Why could he not do as she wanted,
Liz thought, forgetting that he had not been allowed in
before and was therefore only showing how obedient he
was. She fetched a crust of bread and with that managed
to catch him and carry him into the house, closing the door
quickly and relocking it. Billy gulped his crust, looking
guilty. Liz lay down on the sofa and shut her eyes. Presently she fell asleep. The puppy nosed around in the hot,
airless room and then jumped up beside Liz, and he, too,
fell asleep.

In her dreams Liz heard Billy barking furiously and the
sound of someone hammering on the back door. So he had
come back! What would she do? She got to her feet and
grasped her father's walking stick. It wouldn't be much
good, but it was better than nothing. But what a noise!
More voices than one, children's voices, and at last she
realized her family had come home. She ran to unlock the
door as her father shouted, "Liz! Liz! Open up, girl." She
was so eager to do so that her fingers were all thumbs, but
finally she managed it and flung herself upon her father,
crying, "Oh, Dad, there was a burglar. Oh, I'm so glad
you're back!"

Fred held his daughter tight as he said, "Hey! Hey!
What's all this? A burglar? The poor fellow's hard up if
he comes to us!"

Liz's mother went straight to the tea caddy on the mantelpiece and poured all the money she kept in it onto the table to count. It was all there. "What did he take if he didn't take money?" she asked frowning. "Is Nellie all right?"

Liz nodded. "I don't know, Mum. He ran down the stairs, and I never saw him. Billy tripped me up and—"

"Is that how you got that bump?" asked her father, and her mother said, "Upstairs?" in a bewildered tone.

Dorothy and Joan were gazing openmouthed at their sister. "What a mess your face is in!" cried Dorothy. "Oh, Liz, I was second. I nearly got the Silver Medal! The judge said I was very good, didn't he, Mum?"

"Yes, and he said you did very well just learning the language this year. I'm sure she was every bit as good as the boy who did get it, wasn't she, Dad?"

"She didnae do bad at all," Fred agreed, but his mind was on Liz's story. "Tell us what happened, lass. I canna understand—why would a burglar gang up the stairs?"

Liz tried to explain exactly what had happened, but her head ached so badly and she was so confused from having been wakened that her story became equally confused. What happened after that was never very clear to her. She sat, trying to argue that Billy had tripped her and not the man, because he was so young, but she noted the look her father gave her mother and knew that they did not believe her.

"We'll all have a cuppa," said his wife, but Dorothy started making a scene because she couldn't go to bed if there were burglars upstairs. Liz nursed her aching head and then suddenly had to dash to the kitchen sink and vomit. When she came back, she found that the others had been sent off to bed, and her mother now took her up, helping her to undress and placing a basin beside her bed in case she were sick again.

Back in the kitchen the parents looked at each other.

"Do you think she really saw someone, Fred?"

"I dunno, love, might have, I suppose, but it's funny the dog didna—" He broke off, whistling under his breath.

His wife sighed. "We should never have left her alone. It was too long—"

"I dunno—she wasna fanciful—"

"We never left her alone before but the once! Kind of spoils the day, doesn't it? And I did enjoy it! It was nice hearing the children. Oh, take that dog outside! Just look what he's doing! What did Liz mean, having him in the house?" The puppy had gotten hold of a slipper and was chewing it in the corner.

"Here! What're ye playing at? That's enough o' that! And maybe the cow's no milked either! Well, she can stick. I'm no searching for her at this time o' night."

He grabbed the puppy and took him outside. The last of the twilight was fading into the short summer night. He took a turn around. A more peaceful scene would have been hard to picture. The loch lay calm and still, catching the last light from the sky. Wisps and tatters of light cloud hung on the hilltops. In the west a single star shone brilliantly.

Burglars! Burglars in a place like this! Fred shook his head and with a last look around walked back inside and closed the door.

11

The Search in the Attic

The boys were busy that week practicing for the shinty six-a-sides to be held in Portree on Saturday. Sandy boasted of being twice to Portree in one week, first for the Mod and then for shinty.

"It's not going there that matters," Hamish pointed out, "but what we do when we get there!"

"We'll beat the lot!" declared Sandy. His brother was not so hopeful, but at least they would not fail for lack of trying. They practiced every day at the lunch hour and stayed on after school for further play.

Because of this Hamish had no chance to find out what had happened to Liz. She was absent on Wednesday, and he had asked Dorothy what was wrong.

"She was sick when we got home last night," Dorothy told him. "She fell and hurt her head—she had a lump on her forehead and bruises all over—and Mum said she was to stay in bed."

"Is she bad?" Hamish asked. She had been fit as a fiddle when he had gone off with the telegram.

"I don't know," replied Dorothy, shaking her curls. She

was enjoying being questioned by Hamish, who ignored her as a rule. "She said there was a burglar in the house, but Mum and Dad think she's just making it up because she couldn't go to the Mod!"

"Liz doesn't make things up!" Hamish replied sternly. He determined to find out what had really happened when they met on Sunday, down by the shore.

But first of all on Sunday, Hamish had to tell her about the six-a-sides. They had defeated three teams but been beaten by the fourth. He had fumbled a shot right in front of the goal. It was odd how one always remembered one's mistakes because, except for that, he had played well.

He sighed and switched his attention to Liz. "What was wrong with you on Wednesday? What happened?"

"Oh, nothing much," she muttered, fiddling with a bit of lichen. "I got stung by the nettles coming up here," she went on at a tangent. "I never thought they'd grow so high!"

But Hamish brushed aside talk of nettles. "What happened *really*, Liz? Something did, for you were off school sick for the first time."

But Liz would not look at him. "They think I'm making it up!" she muttered, scraping another bit of lichen off the rock.

"Making *what* up? That silly ass, Dorothy, said you said there was a burglar!"

This was the very worst remark he could have made, and Liz felt wretched. It surprised her how wretched she did feel, just because people would not believe her. Well, she was not going to tell the story again, just to be jeered at. She closed her mouth firmly, but Hamish had no intention of laughing.

"Go on, Liz!" he urged. "I know you don't make things up. If you tell me what happened, perhaps I'll be able to help." She looked at him doubtfully. Would he be like her father who talked of "Liz's burglar" till it had become a family joke? But it would be a relief to talk it over, so she told him just what had happened very quickly. She looked at him then in sudden anxiety. If *he* laughed at her, she would be very unhappy indeed. But he sat, knitting his brow and absent-mindedly pitching small stones downhill.

"You do believe me, don't you?" she found herself saying.

He turned to face her. "Of course I believe you. *I* don't think you're nervous or want to make things up because you didn't get to the Mod—"

"Who said I did?"

"Oh, her—" He shrugged Dorothy off, but it wounded Liz, and she was silent for a moment before saying "Well, I'm awfully glad *you* believe me. That makes it all right!"

Hamish disagreed. This was going too far. "It's not all right till we know who was up there and why!"

That was true, of course, but in the relief of having found someone who believed her, Liz was inclined to make light of her evening visitor.

"There's nothing but rubbish in the attic! Anyone looking for something up there must be crackers!"

"No, Liz. I bet there's a real reason, though we don't know what it is. We ought to search the attic thoroughly and burn everything, and then there'll be nothing left."

Liz nodded. "It does give me the creeps, sort of, thinking he'll come back the first chance he gets!" she admitted.

"Honestly, Liz, who do you think it is?"

She furrowed her brow. "I just don't know—I didn't see
him—"

"I know you didn't, but if you had to guess?"

"Oh, guess—it was someone big and heavy from the
noise he made going downstairs—Danny Ruadh?"

"He was up there, wasn't he, when the plumber was
working and stayed behind the rest. I remember you telling me. That's months ago now, but your mum's usually
in, isn't she? I mean he wouldn't get a chance very often
with the house empty."

"Yes," Liz agreed, "but on Tuesday he could have seen
them go off to the Mod, and then he probably saw you and
me going off, and oh yes, Hector went to Broadford in the
Old People's van with Anna, though I didn't know it
then—"

"That's it!" interrupted Hamish excitedly. "That was
his chance to explore at his leisure and not likely to happen
again in a hurry."

"But what's he looking *for?*"

"Money—what else?"

"But Dad got old Uncle Fergus's money! It was in the
bank."

"I bet it wasn't all in the bank. He'd have a 'mogan' hidden somewhere."

"What on earth's a 'mogan'?"

"It's an old stocking stuffed with pound notes."

Liz burst out laughing at such a hiding place. "What

fun if we found one!" she exclaimed. "Mum's always worrying because Dad doesn't bring a wage home every Friday. She says she hates running up bills—she wasn't used to it."

Hamish was not interested in that. "You can laugh," he grumbled, "and maybe I don't believe there's a 'mogan,' but someone does!"

This sobered Liz. Someone certainly did think there was something worth looking for, and the sooner they carried out a search themselves the better, but when could they?

"What about tonight? Your mum goes to church, doesn't she?"

"Yes and the girls go with her, but Dad's staying in with me because I'm not to be left alone."

"Good life! Danny wouldn't come on a Sunday with Hector sitting on the bench outside his door and your house right in front of him!"

Liz agreed, reviewing the situation in her mind. Her dad would read a book, and very likely he'd fall asleep. Nellie would be already in bed. Perhaps she could risk it!

"If you'll hide in the bushes to the front of the house, I'll wave a towel if the coast's clear."

"Well, I don't want to wait in the bushes all evening," objected Hamish. "I'd be eaten alive with midges."

"If Dad's wandering about, I'll shut the front door, and you'll know it's no good, but if it's open, wait till I wave."

Hamish agreed to this. His mother left him at home on Sunday evenings in case the tourist visitors wanted something. Well, too bad if they did.

The plan went like clockwork. Lying hid in the clump of birches, Hamish saw the towel waving before he had had time to weary. He sprinted across the open space and joined Liz, who had a finger to her lips. They tiptoed upstairs together, Liz skipping the tread that squeaked and Hamish copying her example. On the landing Liz had placed a broad-bottomed chair that supported a smaller chair on which perched a stool. Liz shinned up this contraption and clambered into the shadowy loft. Hamish followed, his heart beating fast at the thought of such goings on in a neighbor's house on the Sabbath. He swung himself up just as Liz scratched a match and a tiny yellow flame shone in the gloom. With it she lit two candles, the two little flames burning bright and then sinking to the foot of the wick, where they guttered for a moment before steadying. Liz handed one to Hamish. He could now see that they were crouching over a mound of papers, loose sheets, catalogues, ledgers. "This is what he must have been doing!" Liz whispered.

He nodded, and together they began to examine the pile. Hamish tried the ledgers. "Sold to Mr. F. MacIver, 2 Pol stots, £20," Hamish read aloud. "Good life, £10 a head! They were dirt cheap!"

Liz was lost in old catalogues, where ladies wore old-fashioned skirts halfway down their calves.

"Shake them!" Hamish advised, but nothing fell out. They wasted precious time over this pile till Hamish said Liz could carry it downstairs the next day and go through it properly. They'd examine the rest of the attic together.

They could stand upright in the middle, but to explore the sides, they had to crawl, and where the couplings met

the wall of the house, the only way was to lie flat and push one's arm in at full length. Hamish did this for half the length of the wall without success, meeting nothing but dust. Liz examined a pile of old framed photographs, a severe-looking man in a black suit with a high white collar and a round-faced little woman wearing a bonnet. She would have to take them downstairs, too, and open the frames. Hamish lifted a pile of nets, and they fell to pieces under his fingers, eaten by moths. It was like the castle where they all fell asleep for a hundred years, Liz was thinking, when she heard her father shout.

"Liz! Liz! Where are you?"

"Don't move!" Hamish whispered.

"The chairs!" she replied, and crept toward the trap-door. She lifted the hatch, letting in a flood of light, and clambered over the high edge, holding on tight till her feet found the stool. From there it was easy to step down onto the small chair, and she was doing so when her father shouted once more.

"You up there, Liz?"

"Yes, Dad," and at that moment she knocked over the stool, which clattered noisily onto the landing.

"What are ye up tae?"

"Nothing, Dad." But he was already climbing the stair to see.

"Aw, Lord's sake, lass, ye're mucky. What's yer ma going to say to ye?"

Liz looked down at her Sunday frock of blue cotton and saw that it was grimed all over with dust. Oh gosh! She would get a row!

"I was just taking a look—" she said falteringly.

"May as well hae a look meself," said her father, swinging himself up and climbing through the trapdoor, leaving Liz a picture of consternation down below. She could hear him moving about, muttering, "What a load of junk! Should hae cleared all this oot months ago. It's a fire risk, right enough. Hey, Liz!" He peered down at her. "What aboot a bonfire right noo? I'll throw the stuff doon. Run and get some sacks."

"Oh, we can't do that, Dad!" Liz gabbled feverishly, searching for an excuse. "Hector's very keen on keeping the Sabbath! Mum doesn't do any washing—"

"Keen on the Sabbath, is he?" retorted her father irritably. "He doesnae gang to the kirk then!"

"He can't leave Anna." Liz had that answer pat. All the time she was thinking that if her father got his way, that "mogan" would go up in flames. And then again, if he flung down all the rubbish, he'd be bound to come on Hamish. He had disappeared once more, grumbling because the light was so bad. Liz stood below suffering slow torment. It would almost be better—

"Gosh!" he cried out. "Guess what I've found." Liz shut her eyes. She did not need to guess—she *knew*. But as Hamish made no sound, she opened her eyes and found herself looking up the barrel of a rifle. She gave a stifled shriek.

"It's a rifle," she heard her father say. "The kind they had in World War I. Well, did ye ever! Fancy the old boy keeping one in the attic! All rusty, too! I ken what it was— he wouldna want to pay the licence!"

"He was mean as mean," Liz agreed down below.

"Hey, who told ye that?"

"Oh, everyone says it, Dad—old Anna and Hector and—"

"Ye shouldna listen to gossip!" said her father, swinging himself down by one hand, holding the gun in the other.

"No, Dad," replied Liz meekly, thankful to have him out of the attic.

She went with him to the kitchen, where he examined the gun at his leisure, pulling out the bolt, squinting down the barrel, lamenting he hadn't a pull-through, and then fetching sandpaper with which he began to rub the rusty patches.

All the time there was dead silence upstairs. Liz had sat down weakly on a chair, and she now felt as if she were one large ear.

"Get me the oil can, Liz. It's oot in the shed."

"I never can find anything, Dad," Liz said, hoping he would go himself and give Hamish the chance to slip out, but it was no good. He told her not to be an idiot—the can was on the worktable in the barn. Liz went for it. When she came in, her father was standing facing the door, listening.

"Is that the one you want, Dad?" Liz asked loudly.

"Wheest! I thocht I heard something." He took a step toward the door, but Liz was too quick for him. She flung herself at the door as if she meant to open it but slipped instead and fell at her father's feet.

"Get oot o' the way, lass!" he cried, but she lay limp, groaning feebly. Her father seized her under the armpits and yanked her away from the door. The next instant he was outside. "He'll catch him," Liz thought. "At least he'll see him." But her father came in saying that there wasn't a soul in sight.

"I thocht I heard someone on the stair. Did ye hear anything?"

Liz nodded solemnly. She had to, for why else had she thrown herself on the door?

"Ye got in my way—I'd hae seen the rascal for sure. Ye didna hurt yerself?"

"Not much. Twisted my ankle—that's all."

Her father went on cleaning the gun. Then he looked

up. "Maybe we'd better sing dumb. No use frightening the women, but we'll clear the whole place oot this very week. I'm no haeing mysteries in ma hoose!"

Liz and Hamish put their heads together on the way to school.

"Was I scared! I thought he was looking straight at me. I was crouching behind a pile of old sacks, and I got a cramp. I thought he'd never go! I could see him plain as plain. When he came on that rifle, I was only a yard or two beyond!"

"The gun was a bit of luck for us!"

Hamish nodded. "When you'd gone down, I waited and waited, hoping you would think of some way of getting him out of the house, and then I thought you had *both* gone out, and I came down. I was doing all right, too, when I trod on that squeaky step. I stood absolutely still, thinking it was my best chance. Then I heard you and made a bolt. I was expecting him out after me any minute."

Liz told him what she'd done, and he said she'd been very clever. She shook her head. "It wasn't like that—I didn't *think*. I *saw* myself doing it, so then I did it. It was like the movies really." But though she said this and it was true, she was nevertheless very pleased with herself. She *had* acted quickly and given Hamish his chance.

"But he's going to clear everything out," she went on. "If it was raining, he'd be at it already." Luckily the sun was shining, and her father had gone to borrow a reaper in order to cut the first of the rye grass.

"The minute you get home from school, then you'll have

to be at it," Hamish told her, and she promised. By now she had become almost convinced she would discover treasure. Wouldn't it be marvelous if she could hand over a whole wad of pound notes to her mother and tell her she need not worry any more!

So all that evening she went through ledger after ledger, store catalogue after store catalogue, and found nothing. This time she had organized properly and put each paper as it was examined into a sack. By the time she had finished, she had three sacks full.

"Surely you don't need to take so long over those papers!" her mother said.

"I started looking at those funny old catalogues and wasted time," was her reply.

Liz wished her sisters would not ask so many questions. "Dad wants the attic cleared out," was the simple answer, but it was not easy to explain why she looked through every ledger and every catalogue.

"What are you looking for, Liz?" asked Dorothy.

"Oh, I'm just looking at the funny way they dressed." She handed Dorothy the store catalogue, having first given it a good shake. Luckily the fashions amused Dorothy. She went through the book, pointing out to Joan the funny clothes.

"Let's cut them out!" was Joan's suggestion, and to Liz's delight they went off to the kitchen, where they settled down at the table. But then Nellie came and had great fun throwing papers down the stairs through the bars of the banister. Liz sighed and gave her a pile of papers she had examined, as she did not fancy a shower of pound notes floating downstairs.

At last—dusty, grimy, and tired—Liz pushed the last paper into the third sack. Her sisters took the sacks downstairs, while she climbed once more into the loft to drag out an old mattress, the nets, and the photographs.

When she got down, Dorothy had already taken the first sack out of doors, and Joan was asking for matches.

"I don't know what's keeping your dad," her mother said. "I suppose that machine's gone wrong again. It was giving trouble all morning till he got Danny to give him a hand."

"Danny again," thought Liz. "Bother him! If it weren't for him, I would not have wasted a whole evening over those stupid papers. Well now, we'll burn them, and that will be the end of it."

She went out to find both Dorothy and Joan trying to make the matches stay alight long enough to set fire to the paper, but the light breeze blew each one out. Liz sheltered one with her hand till the flame burned steadily and then lit a thin edge of paper. The flame crept slowly up, found another edge, and inched its way along.

"Oh, it's too slow!" Dorothy complained. "Why doesn't it burn?"

"It'll burn all right," Liz answered, "because the papers are all dry." Sure enough, as they watched, flames licked upward, here, there, small yellow tongues licking everywhere till it was ablaze.

Triumphantly the children ran around the burning pile of rubbish, and at that moment their father and Danny came down the road.

"Good for you, Liz," cried her father. "Is that the lot?"

"Yes, Dad, every paper there was!" and she stole a

glance at Danny. The big man stood staring at the bonfire, his pale eyes shifting from the flames to the dancing children, his mouth open in dismay, or so Liz interpreted his expression.

A spirit of mischief seized her. "We'll burn all the papers, every one, and then there'll be no danger of"—and she paused dramatically. They all gazed at her—"fire!" She laughed and resumed her dance around and around, throwing her arms in the air and leaping high, making her sisters laugh and her father say crossly because he was tired, "Don't act the daft loon!" But Liz refused to be squashed.

"Bonfires are fun!" she insisted. "I like burning nasty old papers."

"That's a good ledger!" said Danny, pointing with his long arm.

"I was never good at ma books," replied Fred. "Let 'em burn."

Liz now dragged over the mattress, and she and her father dumped it on top of the blaze.

"Oh, you've spoilt it—you've put it out," wailed Dorothy as great clouds of smoke rose high in the air and forced the children back.

"It was a good mattress!" babbled Danny, twisting from one foot to the other as if he were being tortured. "I could do with a mattress like that!" But their mother who had come out to watch said that such a mattress would be a health risk. Goodness alone knew what diseases might lurk in its stuffing. For once Danny was at a loss for words. Instead of the usual, "Well! Well! And is that so! To be sure, to be sure," which he was wont to scatter about like a man feeding pigeons, he now stood making convulsive movements of the mouth, but no words came out. Liz, watching him even while she leaped and pranced, rejoiced inwardly. She was even with him now. He had made fun of her father, had let go the ram, had bothered them all winter, had never beaten Angus, and had sold them poor beasts, but now the score was even. She had burned all his hopes of a fortune. Revenge was sweet.

"Wouldn't it be fun if we found money hidden away in that mattress?" she said, throwing Danny an innocent glance. He gave a groan. "It's half gone, half gone—!"

"Let's grab it!" He took a step forward, his fists clenching and unclenching, his face twisting. Then he stopped, eying her askance. "A mattress's no a very likely place— who would be leaving a fortune in a mattress?"

"Oh, you'd be surprised," Liz replied, bent on turning the knife in the wound. "Old people choose the oddest places, and Uncle Fergus was very old." She noted with pleasure how he winced.

"To be sure, to be sure," he muttered while his eyes devoured the blazing pyre.

But Liz took a skip and a hop. "Oh no, no, that's where you're wrong, quite wrong! Nothing's sure, nothing at all! But there was always the chance, and that's why I shook out every paper, and do you know"—she dropped her voice, looking around quickly so that they all stared at her —"I found—"

"What?" croaked Danny, taking a step toward her.

She smiled. "Nothing! Nothing! Nothing!" And she dashed away to the far side of the bonfire.

"Hie! Calm doon, lass. Ye're acting daft!" Her father

rebuked her once more. He was busy prizing open the back of one of the photo frames. He extracted the photo, the one of a round-faced little woman in a poke bonnet.

"My Aunt Phemie," he said. "She made lovely scones. She was a nice body."

"She was, she was," said Danny with a ghostlike echo of his old cordiality. He had picked up Uncle Fergus's photo and was turning it in his hands. "This is a good photo, a very good photo. Your Uncle Fergus was a good friend to me. I'd be proud to hang this in my house." Liz's heart missed a beat. Was he going to get away with something after all?

"Of course, Danny, you'll get that and welcome," replied her father. He took the frame from him, opened it, extracted the photo, and handed it over, saying, "He was a good-looking old man!" For once his echo was silent. Danny, clasping the photo to his chest, went off abruptly without leavetaking. Fred looked after him in surprise.

"Well, now, would ye believe it! He must have been real fond of the old boy to go off withoot his tea! He's upset, poor fellow!"

12

Hamish's Plan

The summer term ended in a blaze of glory for Liz. She was not only top student in the school; she had also won sufficient races against a neighboring school to ensure that Paible won the Challenge Cup on Sports Day. When she walked up to receive her prizes, the whole school cheered her, the boys of her own class leading the applause. She walked back to her seat smiling and flushed, the prize books clasped in her arms.

The holidays! Liz had pictured days of swimming and of going off, a book under her arm, to a favorite corner and reading peacefully for hours on end. The reality was different. Her mother decided to paint the bedrooms that she had not been able to do before because of Nellie, as she would have covered herself and the whole neighborhood with paint, not to speak of upsetting turpentine and chewing paintbrushes. But with Liz there to look after Nellie, her mother got busy. When Liz had finished her share of the housework, she would carry Nellie with her up the hill to a place where the burn ran shallow over stones, and there she would sit with her back to a rock and read while

Nellie, with a couple of tins and a few pebbles, played in the peaty water to her heart's content. Liz learned to carry a change of clothes under her arm, and when Nellie had sat a few times in the water, she would take off her wet clothes and dress her again only when it was time to go home. When Nellie was in bed, Liz was free to run over to the Port Mor for a swim. Sometimes Hamish and she raced across the port together, Hamish always managing to come in a little bit ahead. If Hamish was busy, she swam by herself. Sometimes Murdo and the younger boy, Donald John, joined them. The latter was a stockily built, silent lad who never paid Liz the slightest attention.

Liz preferred this treatment to the flowery speeches of his brother Murdo, whom she suspected of laughing at her. Ian, whom she would have liked to see, was always away with the vet and had no time for swimming. Taking visitors out in their boats kept the brothers busy, even Hamish being allowed to take out one of the small boats when his brothers were away on long trips. On these occasions he was very much on his best behavior, sitting in the stern and steering like an old salt. After one of these trips he told Liz that he had no intention of pursuing higher education—he intended to go to sea.

Hay-making came next. Liz and her father put the hay —which Danny and he had cut—into twenty big coils, and Liz had never felt so tired in her whole life as she did that night after raking the whole field. But both she and her father were proud of the result and stood admiring the twenty coils and the grass now growing lush where the hay had been.

"Grand feeding for the cattle in the autumn!" exulted her father. "There's riches for you! It pays to put on plenty of fertilizer."

And all this time there was no sign of Danny. Liz imagined that her clearance of the attic explained this, but she rejoiced—too soon.

One morning as she was milking the cow, she heard his familiar tones.

"Aye! Aye!" he was saying. "A grand idea! If you make a stack, it's secure. If you leave it, it may get knocked over by the gales. Oh, aye, we get terrible gales here in the back end."

Liz made a face as she dried the cow's teats. Surely he wasn't going to stick to her father like a burr when all hope of treasure had vanished in smoke! However, before the day was over, Liz had to admit his usefulness. Her father and she could never have made such a beautiful big stack by themselves. She had been pulled in to help after dinner, to climb to the top of the stack and tramp it down so that it would hold all the coils. She had loved the work, taking the hay forked up to her by Danny and laying it in layers right around and then packing the middle and making it very firm. It was essential to do this or the whole stack could fall. The smell of the hay was very pleasant, and in the intervals between dealing with forkloads, she lay flat on her back. The stack was like a great bed rocking ever so slightly under her, while overhead little white clouds floated gently by. She was bringing in the head of the stack very slightly each time till finally there was standing room only, and Danny told her to climb down the

ladder and he'd finish the top himself. Down on the ground
Liz looked up at the stack with its neat triangular head on
its broad base and felt they had been wonderfully clever to
make it.

For several days her father and she had walked up to the
top field every morning and evening to admire it. "That's
riches, now," Fred kept saying, "not paper in a packet but
food for animals, and food for them means food for us.
Real riches, Liz!" And Liz had agreed.

And then one morning they saw that something was
wrong. The stack had lost its trim shape and had become
lopsided, and there seemed to be steam coming off it. Hector happened to be walking down the road at the time, and
Fred called to him to come over. The old man thrust his
arm right into the body of the stack and took it out, holding a handful of hay. This hay was not sweet—it was
brownish in color and gave off a bad smell. Hector held it
to his nose and then shook his head. "Taken heat. It's been
too green. You have to let hay 'make' in the coil before
stacking, aye, especially when it's sappy hay like yours."

"What can we do?" asked Fred crestfallen.

"Ah, well! Your best plan will be to take it apart. That
way it'll cool off, and you'll save some of it."

It was a heart-breaking business, undoing their own
work, and a lesson to the townsman not to be in a hurry.

Liz notched up another bad mark against Danny. Helping them! Not he! He must have known perfectly well that
the hay was too green, and yet he had let her father go
ahead and spoil it. She wished he would take advice from

Hector who never offered it but would have been delighted to help if asked, but her father inclined to regard the old man as a stick in the mud.

So the summer days slipped by in bouts of work and play. The animals remained Liz's great pleasure. The kitten was growing into a fine, sleek cat with brindled fur. He came purring around her ankles every morning and evening, arching his back while waiting for his saucer of warm milk straight from the cow. The puppy was now a lanky dog brimful of high spirits, dashing here and there, begging Looty to join in his games, but Looty knew better than that and, when Billy's invitations became too pressing, would put up a warning claw.

Then one day their father came home from the post office and said he had seen a notice up for the cattle sales in ten days' time.

"Now for oor six stirks, Gracie! This is the start o' oor fortunes!"

Liz felt her heart sink. She had forgotten about the stirks since they had been out on the hill, but now here they were again, right in the center of things. The following day she and her father went to the hill to look for them. They saw plenty of cattle but failed to recognize their own.

Liz took this news to Hamish that very afternoon at their cliff hideout. "They won't make much," he said, voicing her fears. "The dealers don't want small beasts."

"Dad thinks we'll make a lot of money, and he'll buy calving cows."

"That's what he should have done in the first place."

They sat in silence watching a yacht sail across the sound. The wind was light, barely filling the sails. She scarcely moved.

Hamish turned abruptly to face Liz. "You were dead right about Danny," he said earnestly. "I've been keeping my ears open. He does make fun of your father when he's with friends of his own, Calum and William Ian. If he says your father's good at buying cattle, they all cackle, and I heard William say one time, 'Here's the man who's going to teach us how to run our crofts, and he can't even make a stack of hay.'"

"They're horrid," Liz exclaimed, hurt. "If they went to the city and took a job at the shipyards, they'd make plenty of mistakes, and he wouldn't laugh at them!"

Hamish, looking at the matter from the outside, could understand why some crofters became annoyed by Fred Shearer's constant harping upon all the things he meant to do to make crofting pay. He could see that they had some excuse for relishing such a man's mistakes, but he took care not to suggest this to Liz, only sat pondering how they could get the better of Danny. If the Shearers kept "Money on Four Feet" till they were two years old, they would have a fair chance of making a profit out of them. Suddenly he saw a way out and struck the palm of his left hand with his right fist, exclaiming, "Got it, Liz!"

"Got what?" she asked, puzzled.

"A way of beating Danny. We'll let the beasts out of the top field at night!"

"Oh, we can't do that!" Liz was aghast at the idea.

"Why not?"

"Well, Dad would be mad, and then Danny would just go and find them—I'm sure they wouldn't go far."

Hamish recognized the truth of this objection, but it only spurred him on to think of a better plan. He sat cogitating, his brow furrowed, his eyes on the ground. Liz waited, watching the white sails of the yacht flap as they lost the wind and occasionally looking across at her silent companion. She was just about to say, "We can't—" when she saw a grin light up his face and his eyes sparkle as they always did when he was plotting mischief.

"We'll hide them!" he said. Was that all he could think of?

"Where could we hide them?" she demanded crossly.

"Leave that to me!" he retorted.

"Dad would be mad at me! Why, he said I wasn't even to talk to you about—about—"

"Well, you have," Hamish pointed out, smiling, "and all we're trying to do is to save him from selling at the wrong time. He won't know it's us! All he'll know is that the beasts broke out of the field and disappeared." Liz said nothing but looked dubious. This nettled Hamish and made him use all his powers of persuasion. "Your dad won't know a thing. We'll go off with them when it's still dark, and then we'll come straight back and be lying in our beds when the hue and cry starts!"

Put like that, it sounded foolproof, but Liz remembered the school chimney and the flaws that developed in that plan. She said as much, but Hamish promptly claimed the episode as an argument on his side.

"Well, that proves it! Nobody knows I stuffed a turf

into the chimney except you. That shows what a good planner I am!"

"It didn't do you any good," she pointed out.

"Oh, I don't know," he replied. "It was fun, and we became friends!"

He threw Liz a dazzling smile, but she only shook her head; she would think about it, but she would not commit herself.

Oddly enough, however, she found in the following week that thinking about it was the very last thing she wanted to do. Whenever she tried to consider the scheme in detail, her mind shied away like a skittish horse. She gave it up. It was not possible to reason about it. She could never defy her father in that way, even supposing she was never found out, so it was a waste of time considering the plan at all. She did wonder whether she should try and persuade him not to sell, but the recollection of how they had quarreled over Danny once before was enough to deter her now. So there was nothing she could do.

On the eve of the cattle sale, she and her father were in the upper field putting a fence around the hay stacks when they saw Danny coming with the six black-polled stirks. His son Angus was with him and his half-starved dog Moss. Fred went to meet them, Liz following slowly behind. Her father circled the six, full of admiration for their sleek coats and good condition, but Liz had been looking at Hector's bullocks and could draw a comparison.

"They're a bit small, aren't they, Dad?" she ventured to say, but even that was too much.

"Small?" her father replied. "Housewives want small joints. It's being fat that counts."

It was no good talking. Liz walked away from the cattle. Angus was standing alone, leaning on his shepherd's crook and watching her. She could have sworn there was a grin on his face when his eyes met hers. The grin vanished, but he looked at her in his usual lazy, impudent fashion. On a sudden impulse she went closer to him.

"Do you think they're good?" she asked him directly. He was put out. His eyes slid off hers, and he pretended to be studying the animals.

"Well?" demanded the girl. "*You* don't need to gaze at them—you know them." He gawped at her, suspicious of her intentions. She gave a half laugh. "Goodness! All I'm asking is what you think of them! Surely that's not difficult to answer when you're so good at judging beasts?" Something in her manner irritated him. He scowled, kicking the turf with the heel of one boot.

"If my dad says they're good, they're good," he muttered at last.

She smiled and drew closer. "You know better than that," she whispered. "You're a good cattleman—" As she advanced, he retreated.

"Och, get away! I don't know what you're getting at. They're good beasts, oh aye, the best!" But his tone took away from the confidence of his words till out of the corner of his eye he saw the two men coming, and he suddenly cheered up, repeating his last phrase as if he really believed it. Feeling that he had escaped exposure by a hair's breadth, he looked at her with such insulting triumph written plain on his face that Liz knew with absolute certainty that he was lying.

"Oh aye, the best! Your stirks will top the sale!" Angus added for good measure, leering at her as she turned away.

It was late in the evening before Liz was free to go in search of Hamish. "Were you wanting him to give you a hand with the cattle tomorrow?" Peigi Mhoir asked her innocently, making Liz blush and stammer.

"Try the shore!" said Murdo, poking his dark head around the door. "I told him to clean the dinghy." Liz ran to the shore, and there he was, head down, scrubbing out the traces of a recent fishing expedition, and so intent he did not hear her till she called. Then he straightened up.

"Well?" was all he said, raising his eyebrows. She nodded.

"We'll have to do it."

"Thought you'd come around! Well, now, this is what we must do—"

13

How It Worked

Adventures were fine to read about in books, but being in one was a very different matter. The small things were the bother—for instance, how to wake at four in the morning. She did not dare to take the alarm clock as it would undoubtedly wake her mother long before it woke her. Instead she had bumped her head four times on the pillow when she went to bed, saying, "Wake at four!" four times over, and it had worked. With a sickening start she had wakened in the dark, her heart pounding in her chest. Then there was the difficulty of doing everything silently. The stairs and the doors squeaked; she rattled the lid of the bread bin looking for something to eat; she knocked the tumbler against the milk jug; the key of the back door was stiff. She paused to listen on the doorstep. All was silent within.

Outside, the mist curled damply. Over in the barn Billy, having heard her, barked loudly. She hurried over to quiet him. She'd have to take him this time or he'd wake the whole household. He wriggled so much that she could scarcely loosen his rope; then he dashed off in a frenzy of delight and back again, leaping out of the mist like a black torpedo. But when free, he was silent.

Hamish in the best of spirits was already waiting for her. Adventures were just the right job for him. His eyes sparkled as he led Liz to where the stream ran under the fence in a deep channel. The gap between the bed of the stream and the fence was filled with brushwood, which Hamish proceeded to drag out.

"Much better than opening the gate," he told Liz. "I thought of it last night!" Liz helped with the branches, and soon there was a sizable gap through which they had not much trouble in driving the herd.

"You follow them, Liz, and keep close. I'm going to make it look as if they broke out themselves."

Liz scrambled out through the gap, soaking her feet. With Billy's help she rounded up the stirks, but the dog was so excited that she feared he would chase them till all six went over a cliff.

"Heel! Heel, Billy!" she commanded him, and was thankful when he obeyed. She shivered partly because of the mist and partly because of her fears. She wished Hamish would hurry up, but he was a perfectionist, so intent on obliterating their tracks that Liz was almost in despair before he caught up.

"I thought you were never coming!"

"Must do a thing properly. Danny wouldn't be long spotting your shoemarks or my boottracks or even the dog's."

"We *must* get back before anyone gets up," said Liz, voicing her chief worry. Hamish was quite unruffled.

"Of course we'll get back! You are a fusspot!"

They plodded on, an eerie feeling of solitude wrapping them around. There was moisture everywhere, on the beasts' backs, on their own hair and clothes, on grass and heather, on moss and fern by the stream. The scuffling sounds of moving hoofs went steadily on, and in a half dream Liz followed, feeling, now that they had picked up a rhythm, that she could go on and on all day. They passed the gray walls of the fank and followed the rough track that led to the head of the loch.

"They'll keep on themselves," said Hamish, referring to the cattle. "We're all right now, and isn't this mist a piece of luck? Danny gets up fine and early on a sales day, and he might have spotted us."

This remark, which was intended to be reassuring, had the opposite effect on Liz. Hamish could not have foreseen the mist, so he must have been willing to risk Danny's sharp eyes even at this early stage in his plan. She wondered how many other risks would have to be faced where luck alone would see them through.

Some little time later Hamish went ahead to turn the cattle off the track and down to the loch. He instructed Liz to follow slowly. She longed to beg him to stay with her, but pride forbade. Left alone in the eerie mist, she soon fancied that she heard the noise of running footsteps in pursuit. What would she do if Danny materialized suddenly behind her? From below came the long, bubbling cry of curlews feeding on the bared sands and shingle, and sandpipers sent up their melancholy whistling. But of human beings there was neither sight nor sound. The animals plunged down the bank, and there stood Hamish, beaming broadly, telling her everything was going according to plan. Liz summoned up a watery smile.

"We're crossing over now, the tide's ebbing, and we shouldn't have much bother."

They hurried after the stirks, which had galloped down on to the flat ground at the head of the loch, cut by many channels that filled with salt water at high tide. The river, which had raced down the glen, now ran a meandering course on its final lap to the sea. These were the obstacles ahead of them.

"Take them up a wee bit first," Hamish was saying when suddenly, as if someone had pressed a button, the mist rolled up and the sun shone full on the hillside opposite. The children checked, taken aback by the sudden

change. They were now completely exposed to anyone who might happen to look through binoculars.

"Oh, gosh!" muttered Hamish, and began hurrying his charges across, using his stick to make them jump the recurrent ditches.

"Come on!" he urged. "Make 'em go!" Liz ran backward and forward, with Billy thoroughly enjoying himself. Hamish's bitch darted in and out, nipping the stirks' tails and forcing them on. The river caused trouble, the beasts balking and trying to run back. The children dashed from one to the other, shouting and whacking them, till one took the plunge and half waded, half swam across with the rest following.

"Round this way!" Hamish shouted to Liz, and led her to the foot of the pool, where they could cross by jumping from rock to rock. Hamish was over and out of sight when Liz fell, tripped by a rotten branch covered in seaweed. The water was shallow, and she was not much the worse, but she had lost her shoe and had to search for it under the water. She sat down, poured out the water, and put the wet shoe on. Then she climbed up the bank and stopped dead. There wasn't a beast in sight. She stood gaping. Had the ground opened and swallowed them up as happened to the children in *The Pied Piper?* Distracted, she covered the last of the flat, jumping the ditches, till she reached the foot of the hill. The she heard a whistle from above. With renewed hope she ran up till all of a sudden she found herself on top of a ridge and down below stood "Money on Four Feet" panting and blowing. Hamish was lying on his belly, drinking out of a tiny stream. She ran down to him, exclaiming, "Oh, Hamish! How clever you are! What a wonderful hiding place!"

He finished his drink and then rose, smiling. "*You* thought I hadn't a clue," he said, "but look!" He showed her how the gully rose gently to the southwest but was always hidden by the ridge to seaward.

"There's a sort of corry about a mile from here, and we'll leave them in it. They're tired, and they'll stay put for a while anyway. The sale will be well over before they think of moving."

"Oh, that's wonderful," replied Liz, savoring all the bliss of escape from anxiety. Hamish, too, knew relief. He had been thoroughly unhappy crossing the open, but now all was well, and they could take their time and enjoy themselves. It was a beautiful morning with the sky a vast bowl above them. The grass was vividly green between heather banks that were one mass of purple, over which the bees hummed, adding to the children's feelings of contentment and security. Presently they came to the corry, a deep cup in the hills. It was cut in two by a bubbling stream, to which the cattle went at once and stood drinking slowly after their forced march.

Liz clapped her hands in delight. "Oh, what a lovely place! I'd like to have a wee house here all by myself."

Hamish was taking off his knapsack. "Long way to cart food," he remarked prosaically as he looked for a comfortable seat. Having found one, he announced, "Breakfast! What have you got?" Liz, blushing, confessed she had nothing.

"What! Nothing! All those books you read about explorers, and you don't know you should never go off without stores!" While he castigated Liz, he was spreading butter on a scone, which he then proceeded to eat with every appearance of enjoyment. Liz felt terribly hungry.

"I know you shouldn't," she admitted humbly, "but I was so scared of being heard that I just grabbed the heel of a loaf and made off."

Hamish shook his head. "That's no way to act, for if you've no food, sooner or later you have to find—what do they call it? Oh, yes!—human habitation, and then of course they nab you and it's all up." He was now splitting open a second scone and putting cheese inside. He looked up suddenly to find Liz gazing fixedly at the food.

"You look just like Danny's dog at the fank hoping for a bite!" he told her. "There! You can have it, but I could easily eat the lot myself."

"Oh, thank you!" cried Liz, too grateful to object to the lack of grace in the invitation. They sat munching in happy silence till the last crumb of scone, the last fragment of cheese had disappeared.

"I couldn't eat another bite!" Liz sighed, happily replete.

"Well speak for yourself—I could." But she did not believe him.

He sat now, cross-legged, his arms around his knees, and lectured Liz. "When you are trying to outwit an enemy, you have to plan properly." Liz did rather wish he would stop talking about enemies. It made it all sound so formidable. And it wasn't really; all she wanted was to save her father from making a loss. She glanced at the stirks, which were now lying down and resting after their exertions. They looked very nice, and she was sure that they would make a good price in the spring. At any rate, they were safe from Danny Ruadh and Angus, that horrid boy, but what about themselves? Hamish was now lying curled up in a ball and looked as if he intended having a long rest, but that would not do.

"We'd better be getting back now," Liz said, and when he did not answer, repeated her remark more loudly. He stretched and yawned.

"Well, crawl to the top of the bank and take a look. Never move without making sure—" The end of his sentence was swallowed up in an enormous yawn. Liz climbed the bank, irritated by all Hamish's rules, but to please him, she dropped onto her knees before she reached the top and looked out, lying flat. The sun shone full in her eyes, and at first she could see nothing, but when she had shaded them with her hand, she saw first a man and then a dog on the far side of the loch. She drew back and hurried down to Hamish with this news.

"Where?" he asked, sitting bolt upright.

"Just opposite!"

He shinnied up the bank and stayed, peering between clumps of heather. He came back. "Danny!" he said. "It's his dog, Moss—got the whitest markings of all the dogs in Paible. He's cutting down to the shore. Come on!"

"But you wiped out all the traces!" she said.

"Not where we crossed the river. Hadn't time—the mist had risen."

So that was it! His plan in ruins! And he didn't even look upset.

"Come on!" he repeated. "We can't stay here." And he moved off in the wrong direction.

"We can't get home that way!" she protested, hanging back.

He looked back at her, frowning. "Oh, do as I say. There's no time to argue. Do you think I hadn't thought of this? I've got a plan for this, too." Then as she still stood hesitating, for the word "plan" rang forlornly in her ears, he added, "Oh, all right! You go back the way we came and tell Danny, when you meet him, what a fine day it is and how nice it is to be up early in the morning!" And with that he jumped the stream and ran up the far side, drop-

ping to his knees near the top of the slope and wriggling
the next twenty yards till the curve of the hill hid him from
sight. Not till he had gone did Liz move. She was angry
with him and his daft plans and vowed she never wanted
to see him again, but when she found herself entirely
alone, she panicked and went after him. In the next hollow
he was waiting for her to catch up. "Could have spotted us
there on the skyline," he said briefly, and without waiting
for her questions or reproaches, he set off once more at a
spanking pace across the hillside, which was so steep that
one foot was always higher than the other. To begin with,
Liz fumed with resentment. This was what he enjoyed,
things going wrong and demanding further mad plans, but
it wasn't what she wanted. He had said his plan was foolproof, he had said there were no risks, and all the time—!
But soon she could not think at all. They plunged through
deep heather that dragged at their ankles; at other times
they came out on scree and sent stones and gravel rolling
down at every step. Streams scored the hillside, mostly running in deep channels. The water was low but the stream
beds were a mass of boulders. Hamish would leap like a
deer from one boulder to the other and then spring up the
far side. Liz followed, legs aching, throat parched, her
body sticky with heat, her breath coming in great gasps.
She was so hard pressed just to keep up that her anxiety to
get home slipped clean out of her mind. She felt as if the
mad chase they were on would go on forever and ever. She
had thought she was a good runner, but now she knew
that she had never really run in her life before. On she

went doggedly, now losing her footing, now getting up, now holding onto heather, now digging her nails into niches in the rocks they scaled. Sweat ran into her eyes, and ever in front Hamish ran, leaped, and climbed with the ease of long practice. She found herself hating him, calling him every name she could think of. Him and his plans! A great plan, this, heading for the Atlantic! A wonderful way to go home! They were climbing a long slope now. The heather had been burned in the spring, and the going was easier. Hamish disappeared over the top, and at once Liz forgot her anger and strained to catch up. But when she reached the top and saw a flat, scored by peat cuttings, he was not to be seen. "Hamish!" she gasped out. "Hamish! Where are you?" Silence closed over her cry. She looked all around, noting the sheep galloping away up a farther ridge, proving they must have seen him and the dog. Billy whined at her heel, his mouth wide open, his tongue hanging out. "Oh, Billy, where is he?" But all Billy did was to wag his tail. Overhead, two ravens were wheeling and soaring above her, now turning over on their back and plummeting down, now righting themselves and soaring up once more. But Liz had no eye for them. She shouted again, though the sound she made was more like a croak than a shout, and this time heard a faint echoing cry, and then she saw Lassie come out from a peat bog, and thankfully she hurried toward her. Hamish was sitting by a pool of stagnant water, splashing it over his face and shoulders.

"Cool you down," he said. In the ordinary way she

would not have dreamed of using such dirty-looking water, but this was no ordinary occasion, so she splashed herself well and then asked, "But where are we *going?*"

"Going? Going home, of course!" and he grinned at her perplexity.

She looked across the loch to where the white cottages of Paible, so near and yet so far, shone in the sunshine.

"We're not ducks!"

"No and I'm not a goose either," he retorted. "Come on!" She followed—what else could she do?—but vowed if he went much farther, she would just give up. Next time she fell, she would just lie. She wouldn't, she couldn't, get up any more.

But when she reached the top of the next ridge, the open sea met her gaze, rippling away to the far horizon.

"Just down here now!" Hamish called back to her before setting off down the heathery slope at such a pace that he grew quite small, struggle as she might to catch up. He began waving his arms, and she thought he was beckoning her on. She wiped the hair from her eyes and saw a boat coming around the point. The sight of it galvanized Liz into action. If they could catch the boat and it took them across, she could still be home in time!

This sudden resurgence of hope was almost painful. "Get home in time, get home in time!" The words repeated themselves over and over in her head as she tore downhill. Hamish was out of sight, and she found herself imagining that he would catch the boat himself and leave her. She fell, scraping her knee, but was up and running without a pause. She saw Hamish again at sea level, standing on a jutting-out platform of rock. She could not see the boat, but she saw him stoop and heard Lassie yap. Then he jumped and was gone.

"Wait for me! Wait for me!" she cried, sprinting down the last hundred yards. Then she, too, was on the rock, looking down on upturned faces far below. Ian's and Hamish's were the only familiar ones.

"Billy!" Hamish shouted. "Take Billy!"

"Drop him!" Ian ordered. She did so, and he caught the terrified dog before he landed. Ian asked whether she could jump. Jump! Of course she could, and did with such energy that she would have pitched overboard on the far side if Ian had not caught her.

"Well!" he said, looking her over. "Where in the world have you sprung from?"

It was then that Liz realized the state she was in, her jeans torn, blood oozing down her leg, her face scarlet from exertion and streaked with peat, her hair wild. She sank onto a seat as the English visitors in the boat repeated Ian's question, adding, "There are no houses on this side, are there?"

Hamish replied that they had taken an early morning walk because Liz had never been right around the loch before, and then they had decided to try and catch the boat that he had known was going out early.

Ian, as he poled the boat off, gave him a sharp glance that said, "Not a bad story, but I don't believe a word of it."

"Well, well!" said one of the visitors. "We came out to see seals, and we catch mermen and maids instead. That's something to write home about!"

"When I first saw this young woman," Ian told them, smiling, "she was all wrapped up in a scarlet dressing gown. She had been rescuing a drowning cow—and looked like Queen Boadicea. Now she looks like a refugee who has escaped over a frontier under fire!"

Liz joined in the laugh, but he was too near the truth for comfort. Nevertheless, it was bliss just to sit and let the boat carry her along, while she watched the creamy wake behind and saw the rough hillside that had tried her so sorely receding into the distance. All too soon the engine cut out, and they drifted in beside a dinghy. Ian anchored the motorboat, and they all clambered into the dinghy, with the dogs whimpering with fear. As soon as Liz had her feet on shore, with a muttered word of thanks, she was off, scurrying up the shingle with Billy, thankful to be on firm land, leaping all around her. The visitors strolled off toward the house, having acquired a keen appetite for breakfast. Ian and Hamish dragged the dinghy up the beach. When it was securely tied and not before, Ian looked at his young brother and said, "And now what have you been up to?"

"Up to?" echoed he, all innocent surprise.

"Come off it! You didn't take that walk for the good of your health nor to see the view!"

"Honest, Ian, Liz has been wanting to explore—"

"Oh, stow it! I don't mind your getting into a row over some nonsense or other but it's another matter getting a nice girl like that into trouble over some of your hare-brained schemes."

"Honest! I didn't do anything. She—" He stopped abruptly.

"She what?" asked Ian, and Hamish felt as if Ian could see right through him.

"Why, she—she—wanted to explore! I told you!"

"Don't waste your breath!" Ian advised him curtly, and walked off without another word. Hamish followed, feeling injured. Why did he always get the blame? He had not forced Liz to go. She had come begging him to help her, and that was all the thanks he got!

14

The Consequences

Hamish had a second breakfast of bacon and eggs, which he considered he richly deserved, since Liz had eaten the half of his first one. She was a hopeless conspirator, guilt written all over her, dashing up the beach like a scared rabbit when she ought to have strolled off, casual-like. If she behaves like that at the sale, she'll give the show away before anyone even asks a question, he thought.

He and Sandy squeezed into Ian's car and went off to the sale. It was held at the top of the hill at the side of the road, buyers and sellers forming a ring into which the animals were led.

"How are prices?" asked Ian of his neighbor.

"Back on last year's."

"Ah, well! They were bound to drop sooner or later," said the man on his other side. "Couldn't go on rising all the time."

Hamish picked up this information while his eyes searched the crowd for Liz and her father. As the second lot went through without being sold he saw them on the outskirts of the circle. Fred was turning around every other minute to look behind. Liz had her eyes fixed on the beasts in the ring. Well, prices were proving how right they had been to take the matter into their own hands. Such small stirks would have failed to make their purchase price. With this pleasing reflection, Hamish gave his whole attention to the sale.

Liz stood nervously beside her father, listening, as he told each newcomer how his stirks had broken out of the park—you would hardly believe they could! He had repaired the fence in the spring and would have guaranteed it stock-proof. He was keen to sell as he wanted to buy calving cows. Danny Ruadh had discovered the breakout and had gone after them. If anyone could bring them back in time, it was Danny. He was a good friend. Liz stood, wishing she were miles away.

Suddenly he grabbed her arm. "Liz! Look!" He pointed. "That's cattle—see 'em moving?"

"Where? Isn't it just rocks?"

"Rocks? I never saw rocks moving! Peter! You look."

Peter, one of Danny's friends, shaded his eyes and looked. "Och aye! Them's yours—he's coming with them."

"Oh, good lad, he's done it! How long will he take from there?"

"Oh, they're a bit away yet. They'll take a whiley."

Liz glued her eyes to the ring. For her the morning had been one long race against time. Now as little as half an hour might decide who had won. Back there Danny was hounding the poor brutes along the selfsame path they had traveled in the opposite direction a few hours ago, and here at the stance only a few animals remained to be sold. In a mounting panic Liz watched Hector's three bullocks being pushed around the ring. They were good beasts—the buyers were willing to spend money on them. As in a nightmare Liz heard the auctioneer's patter run on and on. "Fifty pounds I'm bid, £50—come along, gen'lem'n; £55, thank you; beautiful bullocks, you can't lose on them; £60; now then, gen'lem'n, £61; they're a bargain; going at—thank you, £62—going at £62—going at £62—" But Hector resolutely shook his head. He wasn't making a present of his bullocks to anyone. He knew their value and would hold onto them. Liz clasped and unclasped her hands, thinking, "Oh, hurry up, do hurry up!" Now at last it was over. The auctioneer was hoping to see them all again in the spring and forecasting better prices then. Her father pushed through the crowd to beg him to wait just five minutes—he had six nice beasts coming and he was keen to sell.

"Sorry, sir, got a big sale at Broadford, mustn't be late. Bring them out next time—sure to get a good price then—" His words trailed off as he turned away, the clerk closed his book, buyers exchanged jokes with old friends, and vehicles backed and maneuvered in tight corners.

"Doesn't know when he's lucky," one crofter observed to another, not noticing Liz.

"Och, how should he," replied the other, "a man from Glasgow! What will he know of the value of a beast? It's rabbits he's got. They wouldn't have fetched £30." They moved off, and Liz was left feeling justified. She and Hamish had averted loss by just a quarter of an hour.

She hurried off home, not wishing to witness the arrival of the stirks. Almost to her surprise she found the family all just as usual, Dorothy and Joan squabbling over some pieces of dolls' furniture and Nellie climbing on a chair in an endeavor to reach the top of the dresser. Liz picked her up and sat down with the child on her knee. The small body was a comfort.

"That you, Liz?" her mother called from upstairs. "Is your dad back? Did they get the beasts?"

"They weren't back in time," Liz replied, and her mother came downstairs to hear what had happened.

"Good gracious! And now what are we to do for money? I'm sure there's very little left in the bank."

"Prices weren't good—" Liz began when the door was flung open and her father came in. She gave him one startled glance and then bent her eyes on Nellie.

"Did you not get them in time, Fred?" said his wife with a querulous note in her voice. He was breathing hard and glaring at Liz, but he said nothing.

"What's the matter?" his wife asked. "What is it, Fred?"

"Ask *her* what's the matter. Ask *her* what she's done!" His voice was harsh and quite unlike his usual cheerful tone.

"Why, whatever is the matter, Fred?" his wife repeated, looking in bewilderment from him to her daughter and back. "I'm sure you've no call to speak to Liz like that! What's she done?"

"Ask her!"

"I'm sure she was in her bed when—"

"That's where ye're wrong. She wasn't, not by a long chalk she wasn't. Look at her sitting there as if butter wouldn't melt in her mouth, but she was oot o' here today before sunrise and off wi' the beasts so's I couldn't sell them the day, and never a cheep oot o' her but leaving me to tell a' my neighbors how they broke oot themselves! A fine fool she's made o' me—a laughing stock for miles around—a poor idjut tricked by his ain bairn!"

At this Liz put the child down, got to her feet, and said, "I'm not tricking you, it's him!" and she pointed over his shoulder to where Danny stood peering in from the back porch. "Those stirks! You wouldn't have made a penny out of them, and *he* knew that. He meant you to lose money. He didn't go after them for *your* sake—he went after them so you'd *lose*. You ask anyone who knows about cattle. I heard them talking today, and they said—"

"Well! What did they say?" His eyes were fixed on her face.

"They said you didn't know about cattle and prices and—" But this was too much. He struck her sharply on the side of the face.

"Take that!" he said. "That's what you're worth! Listening to strangers having a good laugh at my expense. Ye're so clever, ye ken better than anyone else. Ye're a cut above the rest o' us. Oh, dear me, yes, quite the young lady!" Then he dropped sarcasm and shouted, "What do ye mean interfering in my business, telling me when I can sell and when I canny? You and yer pals, the Macdonalds, teaching me my business? Well, answer me, gi'e us some more o' yer fine reasons!" His face was white and his eyes blazing. He looked like a stranger. For a moment there was silence, the mother and children fixed in their postures as in the game of statues.

Liz said nothing, but she kept her head up and stared back at her father, all her eloquence in her eyes.

When he spoke, his voice was quiet. "I never raised my hand to ye in anger before—it seems I should have—but it's too late." He stopped again, the tick of the clock filling the gap. "But I'll never forgive ye this day's work. Never!" And he walked out of the house. They heard the sound of the engine starting and the roar as it climbed the brae. The spell broke; the people in the kitchen came alive. Nellie opened her mouth and yelled. Hastily her mother picked her up and went to the door. Danny had disappeared.

"Goodness me! What a carry on!" she said, coming back. "What did you mean, Liz, taking away the cattle? And how are we to live, I'd like to know? But that's no worry of yours! The food just comes on the table of its own accord and will go on doing so!"

"Wasn't Dad wild!" exclaimed Dorothy. "I never saw him as mad as that."

"He had some excuse, Liz thinking she knew best. I'm surprised at you, Liz, I really am. You may be good at your books, but—"

Liz could stand no more. She escaped upstairs into her own small room, shut the door, and dragged the chest of drawers against it to keep people out, then flung herself upon the still unmade bed. Safe from the accusing voices of her family, she gave way to tears and wept till she could weep no more. Exhausted in body and mind, she fell asleep and knew no more till a rapping at the door roused her.

The evening sun was streaming into the room. Her mother was calling, "Elizabeth! Elizabeth! Let me in."

The girl sat up. "Wait a minute." She dragged the chest away from the door, and her mother came in carrying a tray.

"I've got a cup of tea for you," she said. "Drink it while it's hot. Sit on the bed there. Is your head bad?"

"No, no," Liz replied. "Is it late?"

"It's after eight, and I kept a bite of dinner hot for you in

the oven. When you've drunk that, come down and—"

"I'm not coming down," Liz said quickly.

"There's nobody in. The girls are out playing, and your dad's not back yet. Give your face a wash and comb your hair, and you'll feel the better of it."

Liz did as she was told. She was so stiff that she could hardly move. Her muscles seemed to be tying themselves in knots. All she wanted to do was to remain in the security of her own room, but she had no will of her own left and did what her mother told her. She sat down in the kitchen to a plate of soup, but when she had swallowed a spoonful or two, her throat felt as if it were closing up against it. Her mother, who had been watching, urged her to try, but she could not.

"Now there's no use going on about it, Liz," said her mother briskly. "Your dad was just in a temper. He won't keep it up against you. It's not his way—though I'm not saying you did right, you know!"

"No, but, Mum, it's *Danny!* He's been trying to make Dad lose money—didn't you see him peering in at the door with a kind of smirk on his face because Dad was scolding me? He wants us to leave, and then *he*'d get the croft. He's always wanted it!"

"He's welcome to it! It was a crazy idea of your dad's coming up here at his age to start a new job and no prospects! I'm sure your Aunt Emily and me—and you know how levelheaded she is!—we talked till our tongues were tired, but he just *would not* listen, so now—" She stopped as they both heard someone come into the porch. Liz jumped to her feet ready to flee, but it wasn't her father who came in. It was Peigi Mhoir, who crossed straight over to her mother, saying quickly, "I've got bad news for you, dear. There's been an accident—"

Her mother at once foresaw the worst. "Is he dead?"

"No, no," replied Peigi Mhoir hastily. "No, he's not dead. Our Ian found him in the van. It was upside down in the Leac Burn. It was the wheel tracks he noticed, for the van was out of sight. You know how deep the burn is. Many's a one could go by and never notice a thing—"

"Where is he?" asked his wife, breaking in on this torrent of information.

"He's in the hospital in Broadford. Ian stayed by him till the ambulance came—he had sent word with a motorist— and as soon as he was safe in the hospital, he came over to me."

In fact, he had begged his mother to go with him and break the news to the family.

"He's outside just now, and he'll run you over to the hospital, so that when the doctors examine him, you'll be there to hear what they say." Liz's mother nodded and made as if to get up from her chair but sank back again, saying, "But the children? Nellie! I can't leave Nellie."

"Now you're not to worry about a thing," replied Peigi Mhoir. "I'll stay with them myself tonight. Liz, run upstairs and get a small suitcase for your mother with just what she'll need for the night. I've got cousins in Broadford, and they'll put you up. Ian will wait with you at the hospital and take you there."

All this time Liz had been standing like a stone and with as little feeling as one. She had gone through such crises that day already that this new misfortune made no more impression on her than if she had been reading a report of someone else's accident. She fetched her mother's suitcase, putting in a clean nightgown, brush and comb and toothbrush, and came back to the kitchen to find her mother saying, "What am I to do? What am I to do? What will become of us if Fred—" and the rest was lost in tears.

Peigi Mhoir kept saying Fred would be fine. It was only a knock on the head—he might even be conscious by the time they reached the hospital. She helped Mrs. Shearer out to the van.

Dorothy and Joan came running up. Where was Mother going? Peigi Mhoir explained it all to them while Liz stood by unable to think or feel. This was all a bad dream. Presently she would wake up and hear her father calling, "Liz! Liz! Come and see—"

"Will you get the cow, Liz?" Peigi Mhoir was saying, "while I put the children to bed." Liz nodded. Of course, that's what she must do. Cows must be milked, no matter what happens. She felt so stiff that she found every step she took painful. This was a sharp reminder of the morning's escapade. She had almost said "yesterday's," for it seemed hardly possible that any one day could hold so many misfortunes or be so long.

15

Liz in Charge

And now every day was long. Their mother did not return, and Peigi Mhoir had to go home to a house full of visitors, but other neighbors came in her place. One brought fresh haddies and cooked them for the children, another a batch of scones and oatcakes, another a cut of cooked salmon, and every night someone came to sleep in the house so that the children were never alone.

Dorothy wallowed in all the sympathy their plight elicited. She would ask appealingly, tears in her beautiful blue eyes, "He's not going to die, is he?" and was sure to get candy and hugs and kisses. Liz watched this in stony silence. She knew that she herself was wicked. She had not felt sorry for her father that awful night, and now that she did feel sorry, she also felt guilty. She believed that it was her own conduct that had made him lose control of the car. She saw Dorothy eating large meals with gusto. Grief did not behave that way.

The one comfort in the day was Hector's visit in the morning. He sat in the big armchair solid as a rock, praised Liz's housekeeping, teased the other two, and let

Nellie hear the loud ticking of his turnip watch extracted from his waistcoat pocket with much ceremony for that purpose. "Blow!" Nellie would puff her small cheeks and the watch would fly open. "Again! Again! Nellie blow," she would cry, never tired of this magic.

He brought them presents of rhubarb jam made by Anna and white crowdie on a blue plate. One morning he called to Liz to come out. "See what Billy's doing!" The whole family trooped out to find that Billy had gathered the hens into a circle and was keeping them there through the strength of his eye.

"That's what he'll do to the sheep," Hector explained. "Oh, he'll be a grand dog when you and me train him, Liz." He was rewarded by a smile, but it vanished as quickly as it had come.

Back home he exclaimed angrily to his wife, "If I had hold of that boy, I'd give him a piece of my mind! What did he mean going off with another man's cattle and getting the girl into trouble?"

Anna said that Liz should not have gone with him—she was old enough to know better—but Hector would have none of this.

"Would *she* think up a mad scheme like yon? Not she, never dream of it. He's done the planning, and she gets the knock while he goes scot free."

"He's not a bad lad," Anna repeated, for Hamish was a favorite of hers.

Hector repeated his tale of Hamish's climbing a cliff. Anna said that it proved the lad was spirited—that was all. Hector went on growling, saying he'd a good mind to go and tell his father, and then he'd get the thrashing he deserved. She knew he wouldn't. He had been backward enough punishing his own children in their youth.

Hamish would have welcomed punishment. It would have rid him of the feeling that Liz had suffered alone, though they had been in it together. Ian, coming back from the hospital, had met Hamish outside the house and had said harshly, "This is your work!" He had been exhausted at the time from the shock of finding the injured man, from his first fear that he was dead, and from the long wait till help came, with the constant dread that the man would die before it did.

When he reflected on the matter later, he realized that no one could say how the accident had occurred, but the words had been said and had gone home. Hamish felt bad —and worse—as the days passed and no one came to tell his father about his share in driving off the cattle. The story was all over the township and beyond. Hamish was generally selected to bear the blame, but somehow or other his father remained in ignorance. If he had been severely beaten, Hamish would have felt better.

He wanted to talk to Liz, but although he went to the house very day with a message from her mother in Broadford, he never found her alone. There was always someone in the way, either her sisters or a neighbor giving her a helping hand. He had asked her to come out with him, but she had refused, saying she was too busy, and she had gone back into the house to resume her endless cleaning, cooking, and washing. Hamish missed his happy, courageous companion of the summer. In her place was this dull, dispirited girl.

Liz struggled through the days, trying to do everything her mother did. The house must be as clean, the floor as spotless, the furniture as shining bright as when she was at home so that when she *did* come, she would see at once that Liz was trying to make amends for her bad behavior. Her sisters were a sore trial as they kept up a stream of demands and complaints like a long-playing record. "Liz, I can't find my jersey. Liz, did you see my other sock? Liz, what's for dinner? Can we have a tin of fruit and cream? Why can't we? Oh, I do wish Mum would come back. You give us the same thing all the time! Why didn't you let the neighbors cook for us? They gave us good meals. Liz, Nellie's in the burn—coo, she's wet! Oh, I've cut my hand —it's bleeding and bleeding. Oh, don't tug my hair so hard! Oh, I do wish Mum would come back—you're always so cross." And so it went on all day, now from Dorothy and now from Joan who was very much under Dorothy's influence and copied her in all things. Liz endured it because she believed she deserved to be punished, and she nursed the secret hope that if she bore it all with patience, her father would recover.

But one day matters came to a head. It was the day the grocery van came around. Liz knew that she must be careful to buy only absolute necessities. She must not run up a big bill when she was in charge. She had never been in the van before, and the first thing that met her eyes when she climbed in was a notice in black lettering on white saying,

"No Credit." She did not know that the notice was always there and that no one paid it any attention. She must buy bread, cheese, rice, barley, and soap. She thought there would be just enough money in her mother's purse to pay for those if the vanman insisted on cash. She could not get biscuits or canned fruit or even the cheapest package of candy. Here she was awakened out of her calculations to hear Dorothy say, "A bottle of lemonade, please!"

"No!" she said quickly. "We don't want it." The vanman paused with the bottle in his hand, looking from one to the other.

"I do want it!" retorted Dorothy, tossing her curls and smiling sweetly at him. He handed it over with a grin, and Dorothy jumped down before Liz could take it from her. Joan climbed in and said she wanted some candy.

"No!" whispered Liz fiercely. "No, get out!" and she pushed Joan down the steps and pulled the door shut. Her face burning with mortification, she ordered the few things she dared, while Joan shouted to be let in. Ignoring the racket, Liz waited for the man to add up the bill, but to her relief he put it down in the book and she hurried away with her purchases. Joan was still intent on climbing aboard.

"Mummy always lets us have something!" she wailed tearfully.

"Not just now, Joan," Liz said. "We just haven't the money, and I mustn't run up bills when Mum's away." In the kitchen Dorothy was pouring herself out a glass of lemonade. She looked at her sister and said, "Well, that's your fault, Liz. If you hadn't run away with the cattle,

Dad would have sold them, and we'd have lots of money, and Joan could have a bottle of lemonade and Smarties, too." The loss of these delights made Joan blubber worse than ever.

"Give her some of that lemonade," said Liz, but Dorothy shook her head. She'd begged it from the vanman, and she would drink it all herself.

"It's not yours," replied Liz, going for a tumbler. "You didn't pay for it." She brought the glass to Dorothy, but instead of filling it, Dorothy filled her own.

"We could all have lemonade if you hadn't done that," she persisted, "and I'll tell you another thing it's your fault Dad got hurt. He was so mad at your running off with the cattle that he put the car off the road!"

Liz took one step, seized the bottle, wrenched it from her sister, and said in a low but fierce voice, "How dare you say that?"

Dorothy backed away. She had once before seen Liz with that look on her face, the night Angus had teased them on their way home.

"That's what they all say," she faltered, trying hard to sound unconcerned.

"Who does?" demanded Liz. Dorothy was by now frightened and wished that she had not taunted Liz when her mother was not there to protect her. She began to whimper as she always did when she provoked people too far. "I'll tell Mum on you! She told you to look after us and not be cross, didn't she, Joanie?"

But Liz looked at her with scorn. "You're a horrid girl!" she said. "You just like hurting people by saying nasty

things. And Mum meant you to work as well as me, and now you jolly well can, for I won't do a thing for you or for Joan any more. You can get your own meals or do without, make your own beds or sleep in them the way they are! I won't do a hand's turn for either of you any more."

"I didn't say anything!" Joan sobbed.

"No, but you always side with her, so she can look after you!" Liz still had the lemonade bottle and now became aware of it. She filled the glass and handed it to Joan. "And this is mine," she added, taking the bottle out of the house. Outside, Nellie was playing with old boxes. Liz picked her up and walked away.

Hamish was coming along the shortcut, whistling to cheer himself up, when he saw a small figure trotting toward him.

"Hello, Nellie!" he cried. "Where are you off to?"

"Nellie walk!" she announced, sweetly smiling.

"I'll say you can," he agreed. "Where's Liz?"

"Liz walk!" she replied. "Nellie walk!" Hamish did not feel that this dialogue was getting him very far, so he turned the little girl around, and hand in hand they walked back the way she had come.

"Liz!" said Nellie pointing. She was there, lying face down on the grass. Hamish was afraid she was crying.

He sat down near her with an offhand "Hello!" She sat up hastily, asking if he had news. He saw then that she had not been crying.

"We didn't get word today yet. Perhaps he'll be better today."

The momentary animation in her face flickered out, and she sat silent. She had not wanted to meet Hamish. If it had not been for his wild plan, none of this would have happened. She blamed him, only being fair-minded, she blamed herself more. Hamish sat pondering what he could say to cheer her up and chase that stony look off her face.

"Mum says she's sure your dad will get better. Why, there are cases in the paper where they don't speak for months, and then they come all right!"

Liz gave something between a laugh and a sob. "Oh, Hamish, *months!*" Days were bad enough, weeks were endless, but months were not to be borne. Silence again fell between them except for Nellie, who chatted quietly herself.

"Nellie walk, Nellie walk!" she kept repeating.

"Nellie talk!" quipped Hamish. "Nellie's a wee chatterbox." He collected twigs and pushed them into the ground to make the walls of a house. Then he scraped moss off a rock and carried it carefully over all in one piece and laid it on top.

"Look at that, Liz! There's a house for you."

"It's a house for the babes in the wood," she replied with a faint smile.

The smile was worse than her woebegone look, and Hamish couldn't stand it. "See here, Liz, don't take it to heart so——"

"Oh!" she cried, the words forced out of her. "It was me! I made him do it! He was so angry. Oh, Hamish! If you'd seen his face when he went out! And then when Dorothy said it to me just now, I was angry, but she was only telling the truth! I'm no good—I can't do anything right!"

But Hamish wasn't having any of this. He had lived with his bad conscience all this time, and now he'd had enough of it.

"He didn't have an accident just because he was angry with you! That's nonsense, Liz. He was a good driver, and good drivers drive well all the time without thinking about it."

Liz's face brightened, and, encouraged, Hamish pressed his point home. "Sure as I'm here, you'll see when he comes round there was a real reason for what happened. Maybe the steering went wrong or a tire burst. And another thing, Liz. When he comes round, he won't care tuppence about the stirks being sold or not. I bet you anything he never says another word about them."

"Perhaps he'll never say another word about anything!"

"Och, away!" said Hamish, jumping to his feet. "You're just moping. Come on! I'll show you where there's some grand raspberries, just up here!" He led the way to a disused road quarry, all overgrown with hazel and bramble and raspberry canes. He pounced on juicy red berries. A small wind played in the bushes and turned up the pale undersides of the leaves. Liz picked and picked and forgot for the moment her woes.

At last, however, she had to go home, and Hamish walked with her, offering to carry Nellie, but that young lady was independent. Their progress, therefore, was a little slow.

Liz's heart sank when they drew near to the house. "Come in!" she begged Hamish. They found Joan setting the dinner table and Dorothy busily cooking.

"Oh, there you are," she exclaimed, quite as if nothing had happened. "We're making you a good dinner, Liz, and Hamish can stay if he likes."

"Not if you're cooking it," he responded. "I'll wait till it's Liz's turn to do the cooking."

"I can cook just as well!" retorted Dorothy indignantly. She was searching in the cupboard for a package of semolina, and before she found it, the milk had boiled over, putting out the gas and causing a strong smell of singe.

Hamish laughed delightedly. Dorothy said that could happen to anyone. She poured in semolina with a lavish hand till the pudding became so thick that the spoon stood up in it. Hamish remarked that he would not eat such stuff, supposing he were to be paid for doing so, and on this note he took his leave.

The three sisters—for Nellie after so long a walk had fallen asleep on the sofa—sat down to their midday meal in friendly silence. Liz had no wish to keep up a quarrel when Dorothy had shown by deed that she was sorry. She was manfully eating her share of the semolina pudding when the door opened and their mother walked in. All three sprang up, crying, "Mum!"

Their mother hugged and kissed them all in turn, saying, "Here I am at last, dears! Yes, he's a wee bit better! The doctor was quite pleased with him this morning, so I took the chance to come over and see how you were getting on."

This reminded Liz of the state of the kitchen. Dorothy had not cleared up as she went along, so cooking dishes and spoons were scattered all over the place, semolina had poured from the gaping mouth of the package left on its side, the milk had not been wiped up, and the pans littered the floor. In short, the place looked like a pigsty. She had often pictured to herself how it would be all in apple-pie order when her mother came home.

"Oh, dear—" she began, and then stopped because she saw that her mother wasn't worried by the state of the kitchen. She had crossed over to look at Nellie, fast asleep, her face smeared with raspberry juice and one grubby fist in her mouth. Dorothy was already telling her mother what a good dinner she had made and offering her some, but she shook her head. "Thank you, dear, and I'm sure it was good, but I'll have to go back soon—"

"Oh, Mum! Are you going away *again?*" protested Joan.

"I know, dearie, but I don't think it'll be long now, and I'll be able to bring Daddy home soon. The doctor thinks he'll come around any time now, and he wants someone he knows to be there when he does. I'm staying with the Macdonalds' cousins quite close to the hospital, and when I offered to pay, they wouldn't take a penny. I didn't know there were so many kind people in the world till we had trouble. Now I'll do the washing. I've got till the post van comes back."

Liz told her proudly that she had done all the washing and the neighbors had ironed it.

"Well, I have three clever daughters," their mother said, smiling fondly at them, and they all felt rewarded, their quarrel of the morning quite forgotten.

Liz felt that she was coming out of a long tunnel and hastening to the daylight ahead.

16

The Last Search

But everything was in apple-pie order the day their father came home. The kitchen was shining with cleanliness and Nellie dressed in her party frock with a large blue sash around her waist. Dorothy and Joan ran out when they heard the ambulance coming, but Liz was seized with anxiety, remembering his last words to her. What would he say to her now? Would he perhaps not talk to her at all?

She heard shouts of "Dad! Dad!" and then silence, and presently her father came in, leaning on his wife's arm. He was thin and white-faced after weeks of lying in a hospital bed.

"Dad!" said Liz, struck by the change in his appearance. He glanced in her direction and nodded, but that was all. He allowed his wife to settle him in his usual armchair and sat there as if what happened next was no concern of his. The family stood awkwardly grouped around his chair. Their mother talked a little nervously and too fast about the hospital and the nurses and of how kind they had been. She praised, too, the cleanliness of the kitchen and tried to make Nellie go to her, but she became shy and clung to Liz's legs.

"It's Mummy, Nellie!" cried Dorothy in her usual ringing tones, and Liz noticed that her father winced. "It's Mum—don't be silly. Mummy and Daddy are back!"

Her father stretched out a hand to the little girl and took her arm with the first sign of animation he had shown, but she pulled away from him and, when he persisted, set up a wail. He let her go and sat back, losing interest once more. In spite of the clean kitchen, tidy children, and all their mother could do by chatting, it was an awkward homecoming. Presently his wife suggested that he lie down for a short rest before dinner, and he went with her upstairs.

"Is Dad still ill?" Dorothy asked her mother when she returned.

"Oh, he's better," she answered quickly, "but he had a bad accident, and it'll take time before he's right. Play at the back of the house, children, where he won't hear you."

Liz realized slowly that the man who had come home was not at all the father they had known, full of high spirits, full of plans, teasing them, tossing wee Nellie up to the ceiling, and always finding something to laugh about. Now he sat in his chair all day, indifferent to their goings-on. It was as if he were walled off from them. Whenever they made a noise, talking or playing or quarreling, he became impatient and irritable. Liz had thought at first that he did not talk to her because he was still angry. She came to see that this was not so. He treated everyone in exactly the same way. Neighbors came around to congratu-

late him on his recovery, bringing small gifts with them—
a boiling fowl, a few freshly caught fish. He said little, and
it was left to his wife to thank them and to make small
talk. Yes, he would have to take care; yes, they were very
thankful to have him home so much better. Hector kept up
his habit of coming every day and, contrary to his former
custom, would sit with Fred, sometimes telling him the
news of the neighborhood without troubling him for an
answer, sometimes just sitting in companionable silence,
smoking his pipe. Nellie, of course, still demanded the
watch game, and this was faithfully played under her
father's apathetic eye. He had not again tried to draw her
to him, and she still kept away from him. While this was
going on, their mother took care not to disturb the old man
by sweeping or cleaning. They came to have a tacit understanding. She was thankful to have someone sit with her
husband and let her feel momentarily free from the task of
trying to rouse or interest him.

Liz found that in those days she was two people. There
was the girl who, the moment the routine tasks were done,
rushed off to bathe, swimming and diving at the Port Mor,
cleaving the cold water with an upsurge of joy, enjoying
the plash of waves on her face or lying on her back watching the clouds sail high overhead in a herringbone sky. Or
she played up at the pool with Hamish and found that she
had become more skilled than he at keeping their crazy
craft upright and herself in it, or they went wandering
through the copses on the trail of wild raspberries and once
climbed high on the hills at the back of the crofts till they

could see far and wide, hill upon hill fading to blue in the distance. "I'll climb them all some day!" Hamish promised himself.

"Let's sail to all the islands and find caves and bathe on sandy beaches," was Liz's plea, and she kicked up her heels, ridiculously happy to be out and free once more, but as soon as she came within sight of home, the old trouble returned, her spirits sank, and she felt herself creeping rather than walking into the house.

One evening she offered to do some mending for her mother, who accepted with a little sigh, pushing her hair back from her forehead, saying she would go for a walk— a breath of fresh air would do her good. Her father, who formerly had stayed indoors no longer than the duration of a meal, now sat as usual, indifferent to their comings and goings. Liz was at the table by the window and busied herself sewing a patch to the knee of her sister's jeans. They were very faded and in happier times would have been thrown away, but now they had to serve a further term. It was a close, warm September evening, and she had opened the window wide. From where she sat, she could see the loch calm and still and gray. The corn in the field below the house was now all cut and standing in stooks. The Macdonald boys were responsible for this. They had come over in a band, Ian driving the tractor with the reaper, Murdo and D.J. binding the sheaves, Hamish and Sandy making the stooks. Sandy could do nothing right in Hamish's eyes. He was always making his stook out of line with the others. Hamish insisted on their being straight, so now they stood like Victorian troops in battle line, and the oats of the topmost sheaf hung their golden tassels in the still air.

"What are you looking at?" Her father's voice, coming out of a long silence, startled her.

"At the corn, Dad—it looks so nice all in stooks. Hector was saying it was the best oats he'd seen this year."

He was looking at her, his eyes rather wide open but with something blank in their expression. It made her feel that what she said was out of place. She fell silent, bending her head over the patch, pushing the needle through the thickness of cloth. She could hear the homely sounds of the hens scratching and scraping in some rubbish and the cockerel calling to them in great excitement each time he unearthed a worm. Her father spoke again in the flat tone that had become habitual with him.

"It was a lamb," he said.

"A lamb?" She looked up, puzzled.

"A lamb—it jumped in front of the van."

Oh! Now she understood. He was referring to the accident. She felt a wave of relief. It was as Hamish had thought.

"I swerved. I should have hit *it*—damn silly, hitting the parapet." He stood up and came over to the table to look out. "That was to be the garden! Some garden—no strawberries but a bumper crop of dockens!"

"We can plant strawberries this year, Dad!"

"Not on your life! It's back to the town for us, my girl. I've made an ass of myself long enough for folk to laugh at. I'll go back to what I ken aboot." He turned away and went back to his chair. The bitterness that he had felt to-ward her he now felt toward himself.

The next day the post came with a letter for her mother. Liz went in search of her and found her in the sitting room. It contained all the family treasures, a suite of furni-ture done up in blue velvet, family photographs, a gateleg table with a potted plant, and esparto grass in a blue and gilt jar.

"A letter, Mum," said Liz, and stopped short. Her mother was standing by the window crying, not in the easy, noisy way she used to cry, but silently, as if she fought each tear before it got past her guard.

"Oh! Mum, is it Dad?"

Her mother nodded, groping for a hanky. "I didn't mean to cry," she said huskily. "It doesn't help—I came in here to give the place a dust, for the dust will settle even when we hardly come in here at all, and then—it's seeing him *sitting* there, just sitting day after day—"

"He'll get better, Mum, I'm sure he will—it takes time," said Liz, repeating all the comforting things people had said to her, but her mother only shook her head.

"What if he doesn't get well? He's not interested, he just does not care, and soon we'll have no money left, and then what can I do? In a place like this I can't get a job cleaning offices early in the morning like I could in town, and there's all the clothes you need for the High School—blazer, blouses, and pleated skirts! If I could shop around, I could get material and make some of them myself—"

"I won't go to High School, Mum," said Liz, making the biggest sacrifice she could, but her mother only shook her head impatiently.

"You've got to go till you're fifteen anyway. After that you could get a job in an office or shop and earn a little." That prospect seemed unutterably dreary to Liz, but she swallowed and said nothing. "Look, Liz, go and see to the dinner. I'll come through in a minute. I don't want your dad to see me like this."

Hector was studying the local paper for reports of the lamb sales. The shepherds had taken the Paible lambs off to the mainland market. Some clubs in the island had done well, some not so well.

"Do we usually get a good price?" Liz asked.

"Och, we don't do too badly," Hector conceded cautiously. "They're good lambs, and they do well."

Her father nodded his head as if he had been listening, but Liz doubted whether he had, in fact, heard a word.

Her mother came in, saying brightly, "There's a letter from the hospital, Fred. A specialist's coming tomorrow, and he wants to see you."

There was the usual pause, and then her husband asked what the specialist wanted to see *him* for—he was well, wasn't he?

"Oh, you're much better, dear! But it won't do any harm to see a brain specialist."

"Oh, so that's it, is it! They think I'm bats, eh?"

"No, of course not, Fred. It's just that they like to see patients a few times after leaving the hospital."

"That's it," corroborated Hector. "I had to go back

three times after my operation. The wife is going over to-morrow for a treatment, and the old people's van can take you all."

Dorothy, coming in, heard this and at once shouted that they didn't want to be left alone again.

"Can you not make that girl stop shouting," protested Fred. "She'd do for a town crier. It goes through my head like a hacksaw."

Dorothy closed her mouth quickly, looking as if she were going to cry, and Liz felt a pang of sympathy. Nellie, upset by the feeling of tension and the angry voice, set up a howl. Fred jumped to his feet and went out of the room, slamming the door.

"He's not himself yet," said Hector gently. "Maybe they can help at the hospital." Liz saw the almost imperceptible shake of the head her mother gave, but all she said was that they had been very good to them at the hospital, that they could not have been kinder.

Dorothy, who had been standing with her back to the room, turned around, a tear coursing down her cheek and said, "I wish he'd never come home! We can't do a thing —he's always at us!"

"You're not to say that!" her mother cried out sharply. "Of course we want him at home." Then seeing how wretched Dorothy looked, she added, "I tell you what we'll do. I'll make you a picnic lunch, and you can go to the Port Mor tomorrow and have fun on the beach—only be careful not to go out far."

Dorothy brightened up immediately. They must have egg sandwiches, chocolate biscuits, wee cakes, and sardines. Her mother promised to see what she could do. In the evening, as their father was wanting cigarettes, she sent Liz over to the post office, telling her to get some candy and bars of chocolate as well.

Liz found Hamish behind the counter.

"What can I do for you, miss?"

"Where's everybody?"

"I'm in charge. Mum and Dad went to the prayer meeting and D.J. was left in charge, but he wanted to go fishing, so he said I could do the last half hour."

"A packet of Players, please, and three bars of milk chocolate and a packet of Licorice All Sorts." Hamish collected the goods and then said, "Wait a tick!" and disappeared into the house, coming back with two large hunks of gingerbread.

"Sit on the counter," he said. "How are things going?"

Liz swung herself up onto the counter beside him and took a bite of gingerbread. "It's funny—it's as if Dad and Mum had changed places. Dad used to find everything fine and Mum was always grumbling, nothing was ever right, and now it's the other way around. Dad does all the grumbling—well, not that exactly—but he *looks* as if everything were wrong and Mum tries to be cheerful, and, oh, Hamish, he says—he says he'll go back to the city, that it's no use being here, and Mum says I'll have to leave school when I'm fifteen and take a job."

Hamish nearly said that was a good thing, but he didn't. He knew Liz wanted to go on to High School and the University and that this was a blow to her. He chewed gingerbread and wished very much that he could help. He had puzzled his head over this ever since the accident. He made up stories in bed at night where he was forever rescuing Liz from charging bulls or dragging her up from the depths of the sea by her hair. This was enjoyable, but he realized that occasions for heroic actions seldom occurred and that what was worrying Liz was first of all her father and secondly the fact that they were poor. The first trouble was beyond his power to mend, but the second—wasn't there something he could do? That attic, now? Had Liz really searched it properly? Perhaps if they tried again, they might come on the magnet that had drawn Danny to it in June. He said as much to Liz, but she was unenthusiastic. "I did search it, Hamish, except the bit above the girls' room, where the ceiling is only hardboard. You said yourself it wouldn't hold our weight, and Uncle Fergus was a heavy man. He couldn't have crawled over to hide treasure behind a beam."

But Hamish persisted. Perhaps she had not searched every inch of the other part. "Tell you what, Liz. We'll search it tomorrow together when your mum and dad go off in the van. You send the others off with the picnic and say you'll follow. Then we'll get peace for one last look. Wouldn't it be gorgeous if you could hand over a £100 note to your mother in the evening. Maybe your dad would cheer up and not want to go back to Glasgow."

He was so eager to help that Liz did not have the heart to thwart him. "All right," she said, swallowing the last crumb of gingerbread and jumping down. "Send Sandy over to help Dorothy push the go-cart with Nellie and the picnic. They'll need to go round by the road. But I'm not

going to waste all day in that beastly attic when we might
be having fun on the beach!"

The next morning, when her parents had gone off in the
old people's van, Dorothy ran around stuffing towels and
bathing suits into the go-cart and singing, "Here we sit
like birds in the wilderness!" which made Liz laugh.

"We don't look very like birds in the wilderness!"

"No," agreed Dorothy, "but we can make as much noise
as we like!" Liz wrapped up sticks in newspaper. A picnic
without a fire was no use.

Presently Sandy arrived, puffing and panting with the
haste he had made. The children were ready, Nellie
strapped in the go-cart, the picnic basket at her feet.

"Now you are to take care, Sandy," said Dorothy in her
most bossy manner, jumping in before Liz could open her
mouth. Sandy nodded. He was expecting a scrumptious
feast, so was willing to put up with a bit of bossing. Without more ado they went off, Sandy pushing the load, with
Dorothy and Joan one on each side.

As soon as she was alone, Liz ran upstairs. She wouldn't
wait for Hamish as the quicker she was over the search, the
sooner she could go to the beach. She had a small flashlight that was handier than a candle. Having erected her
tower of two chairs and a stool, she climbed up and over
the edge of the crossbeam. Cobwebs hung from the rafters,
and there was the same musty, fusty atmosphere of an en-
closed place, never open to daylight or fresh air, but at
least there was no rubbish lying about to harbor moths or
mice. She crawled over the crossbeams to reach the gable

end and systematically examined each beam and the slight
gap between the sloping ceiling of the room below and the
roof, but although she shone the light down, she saw nothing. Next she tried the rafters, but they were flush to the
wooden lining of the roof, and no one could have inserted a
postage stamp behind them. She was making good progress, so good that she began to feel more cheerful. Another
quarter of an hour at the most and she could follow the rest
with a good conscience. But what was keeping Hamish?
This had been his idea, not hers, and he should have been
conducting operations. But there he was! She could hear
him in the kitchen and now coming upstairs. She had already passed the trapdoor, so now—for a joke—she put
out her flashlight and crouched behind a beam. She'd give
him a fright, letting out a shriek when he wasn't looking.
She was still smiling at the idea when Danny's head came
through the trapdoor. She could see him plainly against
the daylight on the landing. It was just possible that he
might not see her since he was looking into the darkness of
the loft. She froze like a hunted animal that has no chance
to run.

He swung his legs through and sat stooped just above
the entrance. If he moved away, she could make a dash for
the trapdoor, but he did not move—he just sat. Liz could
hear her heartbeats, loud as a drum in her chest. Surely he
could hear them, too; perhaps he had, for he spoke.

"Are you there?" he said—and, of course, he had seen
the chairs piled up on the landing and had climbed up on
them himself. It was just the silly sort of thing Danny

would say, so she answered sharply with a spurt of mingled fear and irritation, "Yes! I'm here. Why shouldn't I be? It's my dad's house. What are you doing in it?"

"I thought you'd all gone up the road," he replied conversationally, "so I thought I'd come in for a wee look, just for a wee look, you see."

"But what are you looking for?" Liz asked, the question that had bothered her for so long.

"What am I looking for? Well, isn't that just it!"

What sort of reply was that? The man was maddening! She gritted her teeth and then said, "You've no right to be here, no right at all, so get out!"

She had come out with what she had longed to say these many months past and was so pleased that she repeated it. "Get out!"

But it made no impression on Danny. He stayed crouched where he was, facing her, and in that cramped space the effect was eerie. Silence fell between them. She wished fervently that he would break it, for he said such silly things that she could feel superior, but when he stayed dumb, she had time to remember that he was a man, a very strong one at that, and that he was blocking her way of escape. Where, oh where, was Hamish? He should have joined her ages ago, but not a sound came from below. She found herself beginning to tremble, but that would not do. She must not give way or let him see that she feared him.

"You'd better go," she said in what she hoped was a firm voice. "People are coming."

She could not see his expression, as his back was toward the light, but his reply, when it came, was mild.

"People, is it? Now I wonder what people that would be? I saw old Hector go off a while back with your cow and his own to the hill. Hector is old now and not as fast as he used to be. I doubt I'll have finished my business here before he's back."

Finished his business here? What did he mean? What business? The very vagueness of the phrase made it all the more sinister. She could feel herself trembling but struggled still against her fears. What, after all, could he do? In real life you couldn't hurt people without getting into trouble, and even Danny had sense enough to know *that*, so what was she afraid of? She dug her nails into the palms of her hands in an effort at self-control and said with surface calm, "But why do you keep on coming up here in someone else's house?"

Her words touched his deepest feelings, making him lean forward and say huskily, "It's *my* house. It's *my* house! That's why I come."

"It's nothing of the sort!" retorted Liz warmly. "Old Uncle Fergus left the house and the croft to my father."

"He left it to me!" The man's voice rose to a shriek that sent shivers down her spine. He was mad, quite mad, so there was nothing to keep him from hurting her, from killing her if it came to that, for mad people didn't think of what happened after! She felt her teeth begin to chatter, but she must not give way, she must keep him talking, for if she could gain time, Hamish would come—of course he'd come. He must be quite close already, and Hector, too, but he was old and slow.

"When did he leave it to you, Danny?" she asked politely as if it were a matter of casual interest only.

"He left it to me in his will, in his will! Why else would I be in another man's house? He told me he had put me in his will just twelve days before he had a stroke and was paralyzed down the one side, with his face all twisted, and never spoke again. 'You've been a good friend to me, Danny boy, and you'll see I haven't forgotten you. Fergus never forgets his friends. You'll see in my will!' These were the last words he ever said to me. They carried him out of the house on a Wednesday, and a week later word came that he had passed away. Then I knew that the house and the croft and everything was mine! Mine! Mine!" His voice rose higher with each repetition. Liz tried hard to think of some commonplace remark that would lower the tension, but she could think of nothing. She could only tremble and stare at him like a rabbit hypnotized by a weasel.

"Well, if there's been some mistake—" she began, but she had hit on the wrong word.

"Mistake! There was no mistake! Did he not promise me the croft? The mistake was *yours*—coming here! That's what put all wrong."

"Perhaps it was a mistake for us, too, Danny, and we'll leave."

"Yes! Yes! Your father is no use now, no use any more. He's finished, so you'll go, all of you, and Danny will get the croft."

Liz, clutching the crossbeam beside her for support, became conscious that her fingers were touching paper not wood—paper, squeezed in under the beam or into a niche chiseled out to hold it. She could not tell which, and she dared not look. She only knew it was what she had been looking for, and now when she had found it, Danny was in the way. If he suspected she had it, he would take it from her. Her fingers probed while she said, "Yes, yes, Danny, we'll go back to Glasgow and you'll get the croft, but let's go downstairs and I'll make you a cup of tea. I'm sure you could do with a cup of tea." She tried hard to sound natural. Cups of tea were the customary solace of the islanders at all times of the day and night.

Danny hesitated—he even made a move to swing his leg over the bar—when he suddenly leaned forward and, flashing the powerful beam of his flashlight into her face, cried, "That's it! That's it! The will! The will!" He had glimpsed the edge of the paper Liz's fingers had closed on. She was sure it was an envelope full of money, the answer to all her mother's troubles. She must hold on to it at all costs. Danny, crouching low under the sloping roof, was coming at her, keeping the beam of the flashlight on her face, his right arm stretched to grab. She flung herself in pure panic from crossbeam to crossbeam over the weak hardboard ceiling above her sisters' room in a desperate dash for the far end of the loft, though what was the use in that she did not know. She clung to the stone wall as she had seen a rat do in the byre when her father was chasing it with a hay fork. Danny was crossing slowly on top of the beams. There was no hurry. She could not get away—the

paper so long looked for was there. Now he was almost on to her, his mouth open, his tongue out. She could smell the stale, sweaty reek coming off him, and with the desperate courage of the trapped, she kicked out violently, her foot striking him in the chest with such force that he tumbled off the beam onto the hardboard, which gave way under him, and, with a rending, tearing noise, split, landing him with a crash on the floor below.

Hamish came dashing up the stairs. The noise from above was tremendous. What on earth was happening? The first thing he saw when he reached the landing was Danny sitting dazed on the floor in a cloud of rubble and dust.

"Liz! Liz! Where are you?" Hamish shouted. His coming galvanized Danny into action. He scrambled to his feet and came running to the stairhead. Hamish skipped aside, expecting to be clobbered, then thrust his foot out so that Danny tripped over it and fell downstairs with a noise like thunder. Hamish let out a yell of triumph. Oh, sweet to see the enemy in flight, bruised, battered, quite undone!

"Liz!" he yelled again. "Liz! Where are you? He's gone."

But to Liz the noises reaching her in her attic fastness were so terrifying and inexplicable that she stayed clinging to the wall as if it had some mysterious power to save. She dared not answer Hamish. She had some confused idea that hearing him was a trick. He was something she was imagining because for so long she had been hoping to hear him come. From far off came further uproar, shouts, voices raised in anger. She would not move, she would not stir, until she was absolutely sure that these were not Danny's friends come to back him up.

"Liz! Liz!" Hamish had dragged over a bed and was standing on it trying to see into the attic through the broken ceiling. "Are you there? Are you hurt? Oh, Liz, do speak."

And then she heard another voice, saying gruffly, "Where's the lassie? What have you done with the lassie?"

She heard Hamish expostulating. He had just that minute arrived and caught Danny in full flight, but what Liz was doing he did not know.

"Well, we'd best find out," Hector replied, his voice rough with anxiety. "I'll give you a heave up into the loft—"

But here Liz managed a small, shaky "I'm here!"

"Come down," they told her. "He's gone! It's all right, come down."

"How can I get down?" she asked fretfully, as if they had been to blame.

"Come through the hole—I've got the bed underneath. Come on, Liz, it's easy."

At last she allowed herself to be persuaded, let go the wall, and slid downwards, falling onto the coverlet of Dorothy's bed that had been blue and now was black with dust. She sat up, flung her arms around Hector, and cried, "Don't let him get me! Oh, please don't let him get me!"

"There now, there now! Of course he won't get you. He's off with a flea in his ear. You'll not see him for a long time. I told him I'd get the police. You're all right, you're all right—here's Hector looking after you. I'm old, but I could toss that fellow over my shoulder, no bother, as easy as a bag of potatoes."

Hamish chipped in with his share of the day's deeds. "I tripped him, Liz, I tripped him! Oh, if you'd seen him going down the stairs like a ton of bricks! Oh, it was great!" But Liz was not mollified.

"Where were you?" came muffled from Hector's chest. "Why didn't you come?"

"Dad sent me with a telegram! I couldn't help it—honest I couldn't, Liz—and I rode like mad to the other end of the township."

"You're always getting the lassie into trouble and then you're not there when she needs you," said Hector unfairly, but he was too upset to be just. Hamish felt this unmerited rebuke keenly. He flushed and stammered, unable in the agitation of the moment to plead his own cause. "I was—I was—only trying to help and—"

"I doubt they'd get on better without your help!" growled Hector, venting his accumulated irritations and fears upon the boy's head, "but if you want to help, the best thing you can do is to put on the kettle and make us all a cup of tea."

Liz began to laugh, a somewhat hysterical laugh that made Hamish stop in his tracks and Hector resume his soothing stroking of her hair, saying, "Now, now, it's all right, it's all right." But Liz could not stop.

"I offered *him* a cup of tea. I thought if I could only get him to take a cup of tea and keep him talking, someone would come, and it very nearly worked, but then he saw *it* and I couldn't do anything with him any more!" She stopped laughing as abruptly as she had begun and took to shivering instead.

"*What* did he see?" asked Hamish, aching to know.

"Away down and put that kettle on before I—" Hector had no need to particularize. Hamish had bolted downstairs halfway through the sentence. He sat on, letting Liz recover her self-control without troubling her with questions. Time enough for that later. Slowly, slowly the dust was settling, and slowly Liz's shivers ceased. She had sat up of her own accord just before Hamish came quietly to the door to say he had infused the tea and would he bring a cup up.

"Oh, let's go down, let's get out of here!" said Liz, hating the sight of the wrecked room. The ceiling hung low over their heads, the electric light bulb had crashed, scattering glass among the particles of hardboard, and over everything lay a layer of dust.

Once downstairs Liz looked around her as if she had been away on a long journey, away for years. Hamish had put three cups on the table, the sugar bowl and the milk jug, and he had found a loaf and some biscuits. Both he and Liz ate heartily once they had started; Hector contented himself with drinking cups of tea till the pot was dry. Then Liz looked at Hamish and said, "It was this!" Hamish saw a long envelope of thick white paper, one corner of which had been nibbled by mice. She told them how she had found it.

"I should have let go and then he wouldn't have seen it, but I was stupid and held onto it, so when he swung his flashlight on my hand, he saw it."

Hector began filling his pipe, always a long process. "Well, maybe it's as well, for now we'll know what's been worrying him."

Hamish thought it a great pity that Danny had seen it, but he said nothing. Liz turned the envelope over in her hands, reluctant to put an end to hope. Hamish was almost beside himself with impatience, but after Hector's rebuke he kept quiet.

"Leave it till your mother comes home," suggested Hector, sensing her disquiet, but at that she fetched a knife and slit the top of the envelope. She drew out a wad of paper. It was headed 'My Last Will and Testament,' in a spidery hand. Liz read it aloud.

> I, Fergus Mackay of no. 7 Paible, Broadford, Skye, being in good health and in my right mind, do hereby bequeath my house, steadings, with all that they contain, and my croft, no. 7 Paible, to my good friend Donald Ross of no. 10 Paible. What money I have in the bank I leave to my nephew, Frederick Shearer, domiciled in 20 Grove Street, Glasgow. All other wills made by me are hereby revoked.
>
> *Signed Fergus Mackay.*
> *Dated August 7th, 196–*

The names of two witnesses followed.

There was silence in the kitchen when Liz stopped.

"No wonder he wanted to find it," said Hamish, "but why didn't old Fergus leave it with a lawyer?"

"August 7!" murmured Hector. "Why it wasn't long after that he had a stroke!"

"Twelve days," said Liz dully. "Danny told me." The outcome of all her effort had numbed her. She could hardly take in what had happened.

"So that was it!" Hector said. "He was always saying the old man had left him everything in his will, but we just thought Fergus had been having a laugh, especially when the lawyer came out with the other will." There was silence. The children's hopes were shattered.

"Oh, what shall I do?" Liz cried suddenly. "How can I tell Dad?"

Hamish had a brain wave. "Tell you what, Liz, put it in the fire. Then no one will ever know."

"Will you hold your tongue, boy!" ordered Hector. "Do you want to put the lassie in jail now? Have you not done enough?" He glared at Hamish angrily.

"Oh, the children—" said Liz. "I forgot—"

"You're in no fit state to look after anyone. You go, lad."

Hamish went, and Hector took Liz home with him till they could decide what to do.

17

A Young Person

Hector settled Liz comfortably in an old armchair. "The fire's gone down," he grumbled half to himself, half to her, "but wait you and we'll soon have it blazing." He fetched peats and broke them over his knee, putting the pieces around the central flame. He filled the kettle and swung it on its hook.

"The wife will be looking for a *strupag* when she comes home! It's tiring for her, all that way in the van." When he had moved Captain out of his seat, Hector settled down to a smoke. Liz questioned him about her great-uncle Fergus. Hector gave the matter thought. "He was a very handsome man, right up to the end—" he began.

"Was he like you?" asked Liz, who had always admired Hector's white hair and clear blue eyes.

"No, he was dark. There's a strain of dark people in the island. He had a good nose on him and deep-set dark eyes. His hair was thick to the last and not a gray hair in it. He was as proud of that as a woman. I used to cut it for him, and he'd sit in the chair by the fire as upright as a young man—"

"But did you like him, Hector?" Liz cut in. He hesitated.

"Well, you had to be careful what you said to him about anyone, for he'd take it and twist it, and the next thing you knew the man you talked about wouldn't speak to you— you'd be at loggerheads. Aye, he liked that. It—well, you might say it was a hobby of his!"

It was a hobby he had carried on from his grave, Liz thought, making wills and deluding people. She pictured him sitting at his kitchen table penning innumerable wills by the light of the feeble bulb, the shilling bottle of ink beside him and the dogs stretched out before the fire. "He was horrid!" burst from her. "He was worse than Danny!"

Hector did not argue the point with her. Fergus had had some good qualities, and he had loved his sister. After her death there had been only the dogs and his money. He had been a grand hand with sheep and the best dog trainer for miles around, but Hector did not bother Liz with all that. His heart was sore for her and for himself, too. He would miss them all, but her especially. She was like a granddaughter to him, in and out of the house, telling him of all she was doing.

When his wife came home, he went himself to tell Mrs. Shearer. "Aye!" he said to his wife later, "I didn't think much of her to begin with, but she's stood up to all her troubles better than I expected."

"What did she say?" asked Anna.

"Well, at first I was wondering did she understand what I said—she had a queer faraway look on her face!" He did not know that she was seeing Grove Street and the little shops at the end of the road. She could go back! But quick on the heels of that hope came the realization that she had no home to go back to. She did no more than sigh. "She wanted to get the police after Danny, and she would have sent word too, but Fred would hear about it then. I told her I'd send for the doctor. They'll take Danny away to Inverness. I'm away to the post office to phone now."

Liz and her mother stood in the wrecked bedroom, the door shut, and whispered for fear the sick man would hear. Dorothy came running upstairs, saying, "I'll never go on a picnic with that boy again! He was awful, bossing us the whole time!" Then her jaw dropped, and she gazed at the mess, speechless.

"Shut the door, dear. Don't let your father know."

They told her what had happened. Dorothy, who dearly liked a bit of drama, kept exclaiming, "Oh my! I'd have died! You were brave, Lizzie, you really were."

"I wasn't," Liz told her. "I was so frightened, I wouldn't come down."

"So that's what kept you! We were wondering and wondering, and then *he* came and didn't say a word but was as cross as sticks! I'll *never* go on a picnic with Hamish again, and he gave all the good things to Nellie!"

"Go and see where she is, dear, and bring me a dustpan and brush."

"What did the specialist think of Dad?" Liz asked when Dorothy had gone.

"He was ever so kind. I told him it was just like having a stranger in the house! Oh, he said it was often like that,

but it would come right in the end, only not to worry him
about anything, so we mustn't tell him about this. He always thought such a lot of Danny, we'll need to keep it
from him."

"We'll have to keep this door shut then," said Liz. They
decided not to tell Dorothy what was in the new will for
fear she'd come out with it in front of her father.

Meantime, the doctor had gone to see Danny, but he had
disappeared. He had been home, his wife said, in a terrible
state, with a split lip and his face all bruises. People would
pay for it, the state he was in! She had gone to look for
ointment, and when she came back, he had gone. The doctor went home. When night came and Danny was still
missing, a search party was organized. The moon was
nearly full, and by its light the crofters combed the hills
and moor. The older men took turns at guarding the
Shearers' house. There was no saying what Danny might
do, disturbed in his mind as he was. He could be violent,
and they remembered the time it had taken four men to
rescue from his grip a small boy who had teased him.
Sandy Lockhart was on guard from ten at night till three
in the morning; then Hector took over and stayed till daylight. Fresh men went out on the second day of the search,
but the day passed and Danny was still missing. They decided to send for a helicopter if by noon on the third day he
was still at large. His wife had hysterics, saying they were
all in league against them. She shrieked and tore her hair
and frightened her neighbors so much that they sent for
the district nurse to calm her down. Ian and Murdo were
out the following morning searching the upper reaches of

the Gask burn when they came upon Danny suddenly behind a boulder. It was hard to say who was the more surprised. Ian found his tongue first. "Come on!" he said in a
matter-of-fact voice. "You must be hungry, Danny. Mum
will give you breakfast. We're hungry ourselves." Without a word the man walked with them down the hill. Peigi
Mhoir was nervous, but with the men there, she gave him
breakfast, and by the time he had finished wolfing it down,
the doctor and ambulance were at the door.

"Well, Danny," said the doctor cheerfully, "you and me
will go for a ride." They wondered whether, his hunger
satisfied, he would make a dash for it. For a moment it
looked like it. He moved his head from right to left and
back again, his pale eyes flitting from face to face, but he
moved toward the door, saying, "Yes, yes, doctor, you and
me—" and he gave a little tee-hee of a laugh. The un-
gainly, dirty, tattered bulk of a man shambled out of the
kitchen and into the ambulance. Danny had gone.

The whole township felt a wave of relief. Ian and
Murdo slept the round of the clock after two nights on the
hill. Hamish and Sandy were kicking themselves when
they found that they had missed Danny's last breakfast.
They had slept in that morning.

Danny might be safely away, but Liz was a prey to
nightmares. Old Uncle Fergus came into these. He was
writing his will in favor of Danny. Liz seized his hand and
tried to force him to cross out Danny's name and put her
father's instead. His hand, the pen, the paper grew bigger
and bigger till they filled the room, and she awoke, shud-
dering, only to lie picturing the old man crawling overhead

with the will in his hand, thrusting it into the niche behind
the beam and crawling away again, chuckling to himself.
In daylight she shook off these fantasies but could not
shake off the feeling that the house itself was alien, not
their house any more but Danny's. She expected Danny's
slatternly wife to arrive at any moment and tell them to
go.

She found herself as many outside jobs as possible, for
inside the house the damaged room became an obsession,
and there was always someone running upstairs to make
sure the door was really closed. Their father was growing
more restless and would wander from room to room aim-
lessly, and sometimes he would go upstairs. When he did
that, the whole family stopped what they were doing to
listen and only went on when they could hear him go into
his own room. But of course they could not conceal the
damaged room indefinitely and one day their father for no
particular reason walked into it. He asked what had happened.

"Oh, I told them to keep that door shut!" exclaimed his
wife. He stared at her, going slowly over the implications
of such a remark.

"Why?" was all he said, but no one answered.

"What's the matter?" he pursued irritably. "Why don't
you say what happened? Did the ceiling just fall down?"
If his wife had said yes at once, he would have believed
her, but she didn't, and he knew that they were concealing
something from him.

"It's my hoose," he stated. "I've a right to ken what's
daeing."

But that was just what it wasn't, Liz thought—it was not his house any more. "There was an accident," she heard her mother say. "They were up in the loft, and the ceiling gave way. That part was never finished properly, not lined with wood I mean, and so—"

"Never mind about that—*who* was in the loft?" There was no help for it now, but it was like being dragged inch by inch to the edge of a precipice, Liz thought.

"Liz went up to see if she could find money," her mother went on more firmly. "Old people often hide things in very odd places. Danny Ross followed her up. He scared her, and she ran over to the far end of the house, and he followed and went through."

Dorothy looked as if she were going to burst out with a more colorful version of the story, but Liz hushed her. They must not irritate him—the doctor had made that very plain. Their father frowned, passing a hand over his brow as if it hurt. "I—I—don't rightly understand. What was Danny daeing in the loft?"

"Likely he was looking for something, too. He was before, when we went to the Mod festival, but he—he—hasn't been very well since."

There! She had done the best she could, toned down the whole affair till no one could be upset by it. "Set the table, Dorothy. Liz, wipe Nellie's face and hands. She's as black as—"

"No, no, wait a minute. I want to get to the bottom of this. Sit doon. What scared Liz? Danny was always a good friend to us and—"

"What business had he in our loft?" snapped his wife,

her patience wearing thin. "And he wouldn't go when she asked him. He's not right in the head. They've taken him to the asylum."

Joan came running in with the letters, handing a long envelope to her father. He kept turning it in his hands as he said, "Danny in the asylum? Ye're joking!"

His wife closed her mouth with a snap and went on preparing dinner. He opened his letter, reading it slowly. Liz came back from cleaning Nellie, and he handed it to her, saying, "Read it aloud, Liz. Maybe your ma kens what it's al' aboot, but I dinny! I'm no master in my own hoose, it seems!"

Liz read, "Sir: It has come to our knowledge that you have in your possession a document of vital importance to our client, Mr. Donald Ross, and we would be grateful if you would hand over this document to our junior partner, Mr. Budge, who will give himself the pleasure of calling upon you tomorrow afternoon. We are, yours respectfully, Budge, Willis and Budge, Solicitors, Portree."

"This is it," Liz said to herself. Now they will come and take the house away from us, and at once everything in it became dear to her, even the tumbledown porch. What would happen to Looty and Billy when they were forced to go?

"Doc-u-ment," repeated her father, still pondering the letter. "I'm to hand over a doc-u-ment I've never seen to this lawyer chap from Portree. I doot he's making a journey for nothing!"

There came a loud rap at the front door. "Goodness!

What next?" exclaimed her mother nervously. "Go and see what it is, Liz."

Liz came back to say it was Mr. Budge. She had put him in the sitting room.

"You're not well, Fred," said her mother, nervously twisting her apron. "I'll tell him to come back when you're better—"

But her husband had gotten to his feet, and it struck Liz even in that anxious moment that he looked more alive, more like himself than he'd been since the accident. But then he hesitated. "Better come in with me, Grace. I'm slower than I was—he could bamboozle me."

Her mother beckoned to Liz to come, too, and told Dorothy to look after Nellie. "If only I'd given the room a thorough cleaning this week, but I'm right behindhand with the housework!" she whispered to Liz.

Mr. Budge was a precise, dapper little man in a dark suit. He rose from the chair, his eyes gleaming through pince-nez.

"Mr. Shearer? Glad to meet you. My firm informed you, I believe, that I was coming. My name is Budge."

"Ye're to come tomorrow," said Fred.

Mr. Budge was a shade put out. "May I see the letter?" he inquired.

"Dae ye think I canny read?" retorted Fred.

"Not at all, not at all! Clerks nowadays—very careless!"

Fred waited for the next move. He had always rather liked a game of chess. Mr. Budge resumed. "Be that as it may, the reason for my visit is very simple. We, that is, my

firm, wish you to hand over the document that was found
by—ah, I presume, this young person—and that belongs
to my client, Mr. Ross." Liz could feel her father stiffen.

"Doc-u-ment!" he repeated slowly. "There's a wheen
talk aboot this doc-u-ment, but I've never clapped eyes on
it."

Mr. Budge leaned forward. "The document in question
belongs to my client. Mr. Ross."

"Well, why should I ha'e it? He'll ha'e it himself."

Liz and her mother were sitting on tenterhooks, Mrs.
Shearer half thinking that Fred should treat the gentleman
with more respect but Liz delighted to find her father
fighting back, her only fear being that he would relapse
into apathy if he knew—*when* he knew rather—that the
document did concern Danny and was in the drawer not
three feet from where he sat.

"That is just the point, Mr. Shearer, the difficulty if I
may say so. My client informs us that the document is here
and that your daughter, this young person no doubt, took
it from him."

"Did you?" her father asked her.

She shook her head. "*I* had it. He tried to take it from
me!"

"Ah!" said Fred, and that was all. A heavy silence en-
trapped the human beings in that room in which the buzz
of a bluebottle against the closed window sounded loudly.
At length Mr. Budge, with a small deprecating cough,
said, "Ah! She has now confessed to the existence of the
document in question. I must warn you, Mr. Shearer, that

if you refuse to cooperate, we shall have to resort, most unwillingly, of course, to court action."

Mrs. Shearer gasped. Mr. Budge had achieved the proper effect in that quarter, but Fred's eyes flashed as he got to his feet.

"Just you come up here, Mr. Budge, and you, too, Grace and Elizabeth. Come upstairs with me."

"This is totally unnecessary—" Mr. Budge began, but Fred cut him short.

"I'm telling *you* what's necessary, not you me. Come along!"

"Oh dear," thought his wife, "I haven't even made the beds yet! What will he think?" It wasn't the thing at all to go asking strangers upstairs just like that!

But Fred, unheeding, flung open the bedroom door. "There!" he exclaimed. "That's what your *client* did!"

"I don't quite understand—" murmured Mr. Budge, gazing at the sagging cardboard ceiling.

"Is that so? Did your client no tell ye he was trespassing and came through my roof? What? He didny tell ye? Well, now, you tell him frae me that I'm going to sue for illegal entry, for frightening my daughter, and for making a hole in my ceiling by falling through from the attic where he hadna any business to be! A young person, you called her? Wasnae that the word ye used? Well, I think that will be the worst item in the list when it comes before the sheriff. She's a minor, and molesting minors is no regarded lightly by the law!"

Mr. Budge was thrown completely out of his stride by

these disclosures. He was badly flustered or he would not have said what he did. "As to that, Mr. Shearer, we have only your daughter's word for all this."

"My daughter doesn't tell lies," said Fred, and, "Our two neighbors saw him," said his wife.

"Two witnesses!" said Fred.

Mr. Budge had had enough. He retreated toward the stairhead.

"You will hear from us, Mr. Shearer," was the best he could find to say as he hurried down.

"Ye'll be hearing from my lawyer, too!" shouted Fred as the front door slammed.

In the sudden calm they heard Dorothy open the kitchen door. "Has he gone?" she asked. "We're hungry."

"We've routed him, we've sent him off wi' a flea in his lug—that's the sum of it!" Fred came down with the light of victory in his eyes.

"Oh, Dad, you were wonderful," cried Liz. Having gotten him back, she felt she could stand anything. Her father gave her a hug.

"Did ye think I was going to stand by and let the likes o' him call my daughter 'a young person'? It's a phrase I canny abide, never could. He doesnae need to come here talking of 'young persons.' He got mair than he bargained for, did he no, Liz, the jumped-up jackanapes!"

"That's all very well, Fred," broke in his wife, "but all your talk won't make the house ours!"

"What!" he said and sat down suddenly.

"Well, now," she exclaimed, stricken with compunction, "I didn't mean—the doctors said—"

"Oh, blow the doctors! I've stood up tae him, so I can stand up tae this, too. What is it?"

"It's the document, Fred, the one the fuss is about—"

"Well?"

"Oh dear! I can't—it's a will, your uncle's will, and it leaves—it leaves everything to Danny!"

Fred's face lost its color; he crumpled in the chair.

"Oh, now I knew what would happen! It's been too much for you. I'll make you a cup of tea." The children stood silent, awestruck by the occasion and its effect on their father.

After a little he made an effort to understand. "My Uncle Fergus made a will leaving everything to Danny?" They nodded.

"It was in the loft," Liz explained. "Danny knew it was somewhere because Uncle Fergus had told him he'd left him the croft. That's why he was always hanging around."

"That's why he was always hanging around!" Fred repeated, staring bleakly at Liz. "And I thought he did it for the love o' me! Who's the sucker now?" He was ashen-colored, all fight gone out of him. He put his hands to his head and groaned. "That lamb! I'll never be the same."

"There now!" cried his wife. "You'll be all right. Here's a nice hot cup of tea and two aspirins, and when you've had that, you must lie down. All this excitement's not good for you." He obeyed meekly, sipping the hot tea, but when he had drained the cup, he told them to bring him the document. When it was brought, he sat there with the envelope in his hands but made no move to take out the will. Liz's heart contracted with pity for him.

"It's all Uncle Fergus's fault!" she burst out. "He liked putting people at loggerheads, and he was always writing wills, like other people write postcards. Hector told me he and Anna signed dozens for him till she grew so crippled she couldn't walk down the brae— What is it, Dad?"

He had straightened up and was looking fixedly at her.

"What you're saying about making wills. Was he always daeing it?"

"Yes, yes! Hector—"

"Grace! Get me the locked box."

"Now, Fred!"

But he waved her aside impatiently. "Get it for me! I'll no rest noo till I ken the worst—"

But when she came back with the box and a bunch of keys, he grimaced wryly. "Ye didna need to be in sich a hurry! I'm no so keen to open it as I thought!" He held the box on his knee, turned it over, examined the bottom and the sides, and only then pushed the key into the lock and opened it. But again he stuck and looked up helplessly at his wife. "If—if—it's wrong, Gracie, then we're oot, bag and baggage, and I meant tae make a job o' the place and make a good hame for you and the bairns."

She put a hand on his shoulder, saying, "And so you did, Fred. It's not your fault."

He shook himself, rummaged in the box, and took out a long envelope. Inside was a thick parchment with the name of a firm of lawyers at the top. "That's it, Liz," he said, handing it to her, and turned his head away.

"Will I read it, Dad?"

"No, no, just the date, the date, that's a' that matters."

Liz read out the date. "August 17, Dad."

"August 17!" her father repeated. "He fell ill shortly after that, did he no? He hadna much time—" Suddenly he stretched out his hand for the other will, the one from the attic, opened it with trembling, clumsy fingers, searched for the date, and let out a yell of triumph. "August 7! August 7. Just ten days earlier! The old rascal! Changed his mind just in time for us! If he'd lived longer, he'd maybe ha'e changed it again!"

He sprang out of his seat, seized Liz around the waist, and waltzed her around, sending the tea cup flying onto the floor and the aspirin bottle after it.

"Dad!" cried his wife, but the children clapped their hands and burst out laughing. Then he staggered and but for his wife and Liz would have fallen.

"If I ever!" scolded his wife. "Are you clean out of your mind? And the doctors telling me to keep you quiet!"

"Baloney!" he panted. "The quieter I was, the worse I felt! I tell ye what, Grace—I owe that chap a debt! If he hadna come nosing after that doc-u-ment and calling Liz a young person, I'd be mooning aroond like a sick calf, and that's a fact! Now I'm gaeing to start work—well, not today but tomorrow. I'll be oot at the corn, see if I'm no!"

"That's as may be!" retorted his wife. "But I'm seeing you right up to bed this very minute." He made as if to protest but then agreed he was tired after all that excitement. He got slowly to his feet, looking pale and drawn but more alive than he had for many a day.

"The dinner!" exclaimed their mother when she came downstairs. "The meat will be boiled to fragments!" And it was, no one having remembered to draw the pot to the side when the lawyer had arrived.

"Oh well! The soup will be good," their mother said as she filled their plates, "and I'm sure you're starving." They were, and the soup was the best they had ever tasted. Their mother filled a bowl and gave it to Liz for her father. "If he's asleep, just come down, but he's had nothing since breakfast, and very little he took then."

Liz found her father still awake. He propped himself up on one elbow and sipped from the bowl. He was serious now and frowning. Liz made a move to go, but he motioned her to sit down.

"I want to say this, Lizzie, and get it off my chest. You were right about Danny and I was wrong. He took me in, but he didna take you in, and then I was angry—"

Liz tried to stop him, not wishing to recall their quarrels, but he insisted. "Let me say what I want—I'm no likely to misca' myself very often—but I was a silly chump just because he flattered me, made me think I was daeing the place a favor by coming!" He gave an angry laugh. "It's vanity, Liz, that's the trouble—just vanity. I couldna bear to see through a man who thocht so much o' me! So I fell oot wi' you instead. Can ye forgive me, Lizzie?"

"Oh, Dad!" she cried, kissing him. "I was wrong going off with the cattle, and, oh, I felt so awful after the accident!"

Her father smiled and squeezed her hand. "You and me's a pair! We'll no fall oot any mair, and we'll gae and see the stirks tomorrow. It's just as well I didna sell!"

The house seethed and bubbled with excitement, but in the afternoon Liz slipped out by herself, intent on finding Hamish and telling him the good news.

Before she had covered twenty yards, she heard a low whistle, and there, coming out from behind a haystack, was Hamish from which vantage point he had been keeping the house under observation.

"Oh good! I was going to look for you. Quick! Let's go right up the hill, or someone will come after me."

They ran uphill till they came to the moor and flopped down on the far side of a turf dike. Sheep ran off, meadow pipits flitted silently from rock to rock, and the southeasterly breeze flattened the bronze stalks of the moor grass. When she had got back her breath, Liz told Hamish all that had happened. "Isn't it wonderful!" she concluded. "We can stay here forever and ever, and I won't have to go into an office!"

She waited for Hamish to say how pleased he was, but he stayed silent. He was lying on his stomach watching the progress of a beetle among the stalks of grass. With a twig he blocked the insect's path, watching it take a longer way around.

"Do let it go!" Liz said presently to break the silence.

He dropped the twig and said, "Did you tell Hector before you came to find me?"

"No, he came to the house himself. He knew the lawyer had been." The whole township knew that as Mr. Budge had asked Sandy Lockhart the way.

"Well, if he hadn't, would you have gone to him first?"

"Oh, I don't know," Liz replied hesitantly. "He was very good to us when Dad was in hospital, and he was up all night guarding us when Danny was out on the hill."

Hamish sat bolt upright. "So was I! I was! I hid in the bushes at the front because I knew Hector was at the back; he's so old I thought I'd better be there, too, in case Danny came."

"Oh, that was brave of you."

He did not tell her that the most difficult part of the business had been keeping awake. The result of his all-night vigil had been that he kept falling asleep at odd moments of the day. His brothers had mocked, and his mother had feared he was sickening for something. He had had a horrid time, with no word of praise till now.

"Well, Ian and Murdo were out with the search party. I wanted to do something, too. Hector said I only made trouble for you!" This was the accusation that had lodged in Hamish's heart.

"Oh, that's not true," Liz said quickly. "I always had you to talk to when Dad wouldn't hear a word against Danny, and you believed me when I said there was a burglar and made me burn all those old papers—"

"And then I made you search again, and I wasn't there to help!"

"But you didn't know Danny would come back! We never thought of a will."

"I should have thought!" Hamish exclaimed passionately. He was quite humbled in his own self-conceit. He had known that Danny could be violent—everyone did—but no one had foreseen his cornering Liz in the attic. His own plan had nearly ended in disaster. Hector had been quite right about that. But Liz would have none of this. She sat on the dike above him, cheeks flushed, eyes sparkling, the breeze lifting her short hair.

"Oh, Hamish," she said, half laughing, but very much in earnest. "Don't go on and on about it! You said I was daft when I went on about Dad's accident, and you were right, but now you're doing it yourself, going on about the danger and all that. I'm safe, I'm here, and I don't believe you're a bit pleased!"

This shook Hamish. Oh, he was glad, very glad, but still sore at himself.

"I know all our plans went wrong," Liz continued, "and we ended up finding Danny's will for him, but it was just as well or he'd be hanging about us still! Old Uncle Fergus was the one who made trouble, and he liked doing it! But he can't do it any more, and wasn't it a blessing he was so mean he never lined the roof properly!" But this reminded Hamish of the danger she had been in, and he groaned.

"We're staying—that's what matters—and oh, Hamish! Rosie's going to calve at Christmas! Won't that be lovely?"

Hamish smiled. A calving cow was commonplace to him.

"And Hector's going to look after Billy for me and train him when I'm in school."

"*I've* been keeping an eye on the stirks. They might have taken a fever after all the racing and chasing the day of the sale, so I went to see them every day, even when we were making corn stacks."

"Oh, that was good of you, Hamish! Where are they? Dad wants to see them tomorrow."

Hamish jumped to his feet, smiling. "You haven't got Danny now to help find them. You'll have to learn to recognize your own beasts, seeing you're going to be crofters for keeps now. They're just over the brae here. Come on and see if you can pick them out!"

"I'll pick them out all right!" shouted Liz, on top of the world, sprinting away to be first to see them, but Hamish raced after her and beat her by ten yards, which was satisfactory to both parties.